Christmastime 1943

A Love Story

LINDA MAHKOVEC

D1636947

Also by Linda Mahkovec

The Dreams of Youth

Seven Tales of Love

The Garden House

The Christmastime Series

Christmastime 1940: A Love Story

Christmastime 1941: A Love Story

Christmastime 1942: A Love Story

Christmastime 1943: A Love Story
by Linda Mahkovec
...
Copyright © 2015

This b ook i s a w ork o f fi ction. Wh ile re ferences ma y be made to actual places or events, the names, character, incidents, and locations within are from the author's imagination and are not a resemblance to actual living or dead persons, businesses, or events. Any similarity is coincidental.

ISBN-10:1-946229-09-1
ISBN-13:978-1-946229-09-0

Distributed by Bublish, Inc.

Cover Design by Laura Duffy
© Colin Young/Dreamstime

In loving memory of my father –
a small town boy from Illinois who joined
the Army Airforce in 1943
and flew 25 missions over Europe.

Historical note:
In WWII, there were over 425,000 prisoners of war (mostly German) in the United States, with POW camps in all but four states. They were used to help fill the labor shortage, working on farms, and in canneries and factories.

Chapter 1

War and Christmas. Soldiers and shoppers. Fear and festivities. Another holiday season on the home front. Lillian pulled her scarf closer around her neck as she gazed out the window of the Monday morning crosstown bus. A soft snow had begun to fall, bringing to life the early Christmas decorations in the store windows and highlighting the rows of Christmas trees that were lately set out. Lillian's thoughts of war and Charles and the holiday season were interrupted by the sight of a woman walking briskly along the sidewalk. She was dressed in a deep green coat, swinging her arms, full of energy. Izzy.

Lillian got off the bus one stop early and called out to her friend, but Izzy was moving in some happy world of her own. Only when she paused to look at the Christmas decorations in a department store window, was Lillian able to catch up with her.

"Izzy, wait up!"

Izzy spun around. "Morning, Lilly!" She swept her arm towards the store window. "Just look at that – a real Christmas fairyland for the kids." She thrust her hands into her pockets and looked up and down the avenue. "Don't you just love this time of year? Everything so festive, everyone so happy."

Lillian turned away from the miniature Christmas village in the window and raised her eyebrows at Izzy.

"I know. I'm like a kid." Izzy lifted and dropped her shoulders with excitement. "I can't help it. It's going to be a wonderful Christmas! I can just feel it."

"Okay," said Lillian, linking her arm with Izzy's as they headed towards Rockwell Publishing. "What's changed since last week? I seem to remember you wishing the holidays were over."

Izzy reached into her handbag, pulled out a letter, and waved it. "This!"

Lillian laughed at her exuberance. "Which one is that?"

Izzy pulled a face of mock offense and pressed the letter to her heart. "The only one I care about. Sergeant Archibald Reynolds. Archie," she sighed. "He arrives next week for a two-week furlough."

"Well that explains everything. Is that Handsome Kansas?"

"Handsome Kansas? Heavens, no! Kansas got married in June. And he really wasn't all that handsome. It was just that line about bringing me a *sodie pop* that initially charmed me. No," she sighed again, "Archie is the one from Yonkers. Really, Lilly, he's perfect. Funny, charming, handsome – and madly in love with me."

When they arrived at the office building, Izzy pushed through the revolving door, cutting Lillian off mid-sentence. "Sounds more serious than – "

"Than the others?" laughed Izzy, brushing the snow from her coat.

"No, I was going to say more serious than I realized."

"Morning!" Izzy said, passing some of her colleagues. "Good morning!"

This was definitely not Izzy's usual Monday morning demeanor.

They walked through the crowded lobby and waited for the elevator.

"I know it's hard to believe, but I've gotten to know him so much better over the past several months. Sure, it started with the whirlwind romance in the spring, but it's the letters that's really brought us closer." She gazed off blinking sweetly at the ceiling. "He has a real way of expressing himself."

"I'm happy for you, Izzy," Lillian said, delighted to find that, after two years, Izzy had finally moved past her heartbreak with Red and was able to love again.

Izzy held up a warning finger. "And no excuses about you being too busy to go out. I'll drag you out if I have to. I want you to meet him. Oh, I don't know how I'm going to get through another week." Izzy caught Lillian's fleeting look of concern and squeezed her arm. "Still no word?"

Lillian shook her head. "It's been over two months now."

"Well, it can take a while. I'm sure you'll get a letter soon." But her words did nothing to dispel the sadness in Lillian's face. "Look, Lilly, I know how hard it's been for you. Barely married last year before Charles was whisked away. And you've been apart for most of this year. That's rough. And I can just imagine how upset Tommy and Gabriel are. But things will look up soon."

They stepped into the elevator, and Izzy turned to her. "Hey, have you thought more about going to your sister's for Christmas? You should be around family this time of year. And I bet the orchard is beautiful in the snow."

Lillian envisioned the rows of bare fruit trees, the cider house where the kids liked to play, the coziness of her sister's home, and nodded. "It would be good for the boys. Everything with them is war and tanks and guns. Tommy got into another fisticuff over the weekend. Gabriel's grades are slipping and he seems distracted all the time. I think some time in the country is just what they need." Lillian's expression changed to one of doubt as she pondered the trip. "I'm still undecided. Charles's last letter said that he wouldn't be home anytime soon, but I don't want to take the risk of missing him. Or his letters."

"Well, Christmas is still weeks away. You have some time to decide. I'm sure you'll hear from him before long."

The elevator doors opened to the main floor of Rockwell Publishing, and Izzy stepped out. She tapped under her chin in an exaggerated "chin up" gesture.

Lillian playfully raised her chin and nodded – but her smile faded as soon as the doors closed. In her heart she knew that Charles would not be home for Christmas. He was sure of it in his last letter. So many furloughs were being cancelled – fighting was fierce and relentless.

As the elevator continued to the higher floors, she tried to focus on the victories, the signs that the tide of war was changing. The Allies had defeated Rommel in North Africa, had taken Sicily, and were now pushing up into Italy. And in the Pacific, they were taking back the islands that the Japanese had so ruthlessly seized.

Yet the fate of the world was still unknown. Everyone knew that the heaviest fighting still lay ahead. And despite victories, the losses were staggering. They were fighting an enemy that seemed to have no heart or soul – cruel, aggressive forces that would stop at nothing.

Though she knew it was unreasonable, she derived some comfort in knowing that Charles was somewhere in Europe. It was a matter she frequently debated – which theater of war she preferred Charles to be in. Today it was Europe. It was closer, and she was better able to imagine him there, across the ocean where she could get to him more quickly if she had to – though she knew how unlikely that was.

But then she changed her mind when she thought of him in the freezing cold. Though she couldn't be sure, she believed that he was still in the turbulent, frigid waters of the North Atlantic. Every time she thought of him on an icy deck or in an arctic gale, a chill shot through her. She fantasized about having one night with him so that she could keep him warm, cook him a proper meal, fix him a hot bath, and make sure that he had a deep, peaceful sleep with her arms around him in protection. She had spent many nights wrapped in such visions. She worried constantly about the toll the war was taking on him, and she lived in fear of the U-boats, of planes bombing his ship –

She pushed those thoughts away. The best way to keep fear at bay, she had learned, was to keep busy, to do her part for the war effort. She didn't mind that her hours at the publishing house had been extended. More often than not, she worked through her lunch break, and took assignments home. Every now and then, she went to the office on Saturdays to complete an illustration in time for publication. She had a hard time working fast enough to keep up with the various projects, and Rockwell was demanding. But she never minded. The war-themed illustrations, largely calls to action, were a way of bringing her closer to Charles.

Lillian got off the elevator on her floor and entered the Art Department. She hung up her hat and coat, and took a deep breath to settle into another workweek. Scattered on her desk were sketches for a series of posters she was working on – women in the workforce. With most of the men gone or in training, work shortages were severe and it was crucial that women fill the gaps. She had just read that twenty percent of the workforce was now enlisted, which meant that millions were needed to replace them. Millions!

She had already submitted drawings of women working directly in war production jobs, such as welders and riveters in the shipyards and factories. Other drawings portrayed women delivering mail, pumping gas, and driving taxis, buses, and trolley cars. A recent poster depicted several older women running day care centers so that the young mothers could step into jobs that had recently been vacated by men. The only way to win this war was to keep production at the break-neck pace that President Roosevelt had established; he had made it clear that the enemy must be "out-fought and out-produced."

Lillian shuffled the drawings around on her desk. The theme of the next poster series was women and farm production. She glanced over at her drawings from last week of women driving combines and pickup trucks, harvesting hay, and plowing fields.

She studied one drawing of a pretty, young woman in overalls driving a tractor and holding up the two-fingered victory sign in greeting to the army trucks passing by. The young woman had a cheerful, energetic ease about her – though Lillian knew that the reality was much bleaker for most farmwomen.

But reality was not what Mr. Rockwell, or the War Department, had asked for. They wanted optimism, hope, even glamor. Women must be compelled to join the workforce, and what better way than to make the idea attractive? So the women in the posters had to be pretty, with good figures, and an expression of spunky determination in their eyes. The drudgery of work was dispelled by a touch of lipstick, or one of the war-time hairstyles championed by the Hollywood stars, or anything that added charm and allure. Charm on the farm, Lillian thought, lightly tapping her pencil.

She set the drawings aside and looked out the window, her habit when envisioning a new composition. The snow was falling more heavily now, softening the gray of the buildings outside. Her mind filled with thoughts of Charles's sister, Kate, in Illinois – practically alone on her farm, along with her two teenaged daughters. Her husband had died years before, and now all four of her sons were gone. Francis – sweet Francis – had been killed in Tunisia in the spring, and the fate of her eldest son, Eugene, was precarious, flying mission after mission over Europe. James was in the Navy and on his way to the Pacific. And now the youngest, Paul, had joined the Army, against his mother's wishes. Although it was allowed for one son, often the youngest, to stay and work the farm, Paul had enlisted shortly after Francis's death, lying about his age to be accepted.

Kate's last letter was full of hope and determination, but Lillian knew that it belied despair. Francis's death had come as a devastating blow to the family. Ursula, the elder daughter, was taking it especially hard. Francis and Ursula had been close in age and had always looked out for one another. Jessica, the younger daughter, was closer to Paul. Now, with Paul gone, it was just Kate and the girls – and Ed, the old farmhand. Kate wrote that they would manage somehow, like everyone else.

Lillian's mouth softened into a sad smile as she remembered the trip to Kate's the summer before the war. All of Kate's sons were fine young men – hard-working, good-natured, handsome – and Lillian admired them all. A bittersweet sorrow filled her at the memory of Francis. There was something special about him. He was quiet, gentle, and always at hand when anyone needed help. She had a particularly fond memory of one dewy early morning when he helped her cut bunches of lavender before the bumblebees became active. As they filled a basket with the fragrant flowers, he told her about his dreams of going to college to study agriculture, and how he hoped to marry his girl, Maria, and buy a farm of his own. Lillian closed her eyes, and wondered how Kate could bear the loss.

Everyone had been touched by the war, knew of someone who had been killed – if not a son or husband, then a cousin, a brother-in-law, the boy down the street. The euphoria of the early days, when morale and determination ran high, had been replaced by gritty determination. The wounded were returning in greater numbers, and the list of those killed was ever growing. More and more men were leaving, and more women were filling jobs on the home front. Food and fuel were rationed, and housing was scarce. There was less of everything. Except loneliness – that seemed to increase as the months wore on. Lillian hadn't seen Charles since early summer when he was home for one brief week.

Realizing that she was slipping into self-pity, Lillian caught herself and sat straighter. She thought of Izzy's parting gesture and raised her chin. I'll get through this. We'll all get through this.

The Monday morning department meeting ran over by an hour, and Lillian found herself taking on yet more assignments; she would have to learn to work faster. As she returned to her desk, she heard a tapping sound in the hallway and wondered what new information was being posted.

Several of her co-workers went to see, their conversation floating back to her while she continued working on the sketch of the girl on a tractor. Lillian studied it and realized that she had largely based the girl on Jessica, the younger of Kate's daughters – blonde, cheerful, wholesome. Lillian had first tried the sketch based on Ursula, but the look was all wrong.

Again, Lillian gazed out the window, tapping the pencil against her cheek. Both of Kate's daughters were extremely pretty – but Ursula had that elusive quality of beauty. Though her features were striking, Lillian felt that her beauty had more to do with her expressions, her soft way of speaking, her behavior – she was both pensive and brisk – as if her mind pulled her in one direction, and her body in another. No, thought Lillian, Ursula was more difficult to imagine on a tractor than Jessica, even though Kate wrote that Ursula had really taken up the slack at the farm as one by one her brothers had left. It was easier to imagine Ursula as some kind of mythic heroine – Diana the huntress, perhaps, or a winged victory figure.

Lillian thought of Ursula as she was two years ago – setting out on one of her restless walks across the fields or along the country road, or tucked away poring over a book. Her heart was set on going to college, and that was the life that would best suit her. She was intelligent, curious, strong willed. Kate had sent a photo in the summer, and Ursula was prettier than ever. Lillian began a sketch of such a girl – tall and slim, with wavy dark hair, and those exquisitely lovely eyes – deep blue, beneath eyebrows like angry wings, smooth and beautiful. An air of intensity surrounded her, as if a quiet fire burned within.

As the drawing took shape, Lillian frowned at the goddess in overalls. She tried adding a straw hat, and then scratched it out. It just didn't work. No – to capture that wholesome Midwestern spirit of hard work and determination, she would need to go with Jessica. Perhaps she could use Ursula for another –

"Lilly! Come take a look at this."

She saw Izzy poking her head around the corner, waving her over.

As office manager of Rockwell Publishing, Izzy was in charge of the distribution of information regarding contests, drives, and volunteer opportunities. When Lillian stepped out to the hall, she found Izzy smoothing down a poster on the wall. An older man, who did double duty as mail deliverer and handyman, eyed the tacks on the poster and then gave them all a final tap.

"Take a look. What do you think?" asked Izzy

Lillian stood behind a few colleagues in front of the poster and read: "Artists for Victory."

"Right up your line," said Izzy.

"Another contest?" Lillian asked, remembering her disappointment at last year's government sponsored contest in which she hadn't even placed.

"No," said one of the other artists, reading the print. "Not a contest. They're asking for volunteers." She ran her finger under the description, reading out key phrases: "'teach drawing and painting at hospitals and USO locations . . . make sketches of the servicemen to send home to their loved ones.'"

Lillian turned to Izzy. "I could do that." She leaned forward to read the various locations.

"Look – this hospital is not so far away. I would like to help out with the wounded. I could go on one of the nights that Tommy and Gabriel have Boy Scouts."

Izzy gave a firm nod. "It would be good for you to get out."

Lillian shot her a quick look, wondering if that was the motive behind Izzy's encouragement.

"And," Izzy quickly added, "you'd be helping out our men."

Izzy was forever trying to get Lillian to go out – to the dances, the shows, to get dressed up and have some fun. But Lillian always turned her down, saying that she had work to do, or just that she wanted to be home with her boys.

Lillian crossed her arms, considering the logistics. "I'll speak to Mrs. Kuntzman. See if she could watch the boys after Scouts. Tommy won't be happy about it. He insists he's too old to have a babysitter. But Gabriel's too young to be without supervision."

"What is he, eight?"

"Nine! And Tommy's almost thirteen. Once in a while I let them go straight home from school rather than stopping by Mrs. Kuntzman's. A sort of trial run without a babysitter. But they're often out on weeknights with the Boy Scouts doing scrap drives, delivering posters and leaflets, planning

Christmas activities. Maybe I can arrange to volunteer on the same nights."

"Of course you can! I'd join myself, but between my late nights here, the Stage Door Canteen, the USO drives and" – she stopped to pat her hair – "my social life, my nights are booked. Besides, I can't even draw a straight line."

Lillian liked the idea of helping the GIs on an individual basis. She'd been knitting caps and scarves for the sailors on the North Sea, and periodically she went with her neighbor Mrs. Wilson, to help out at the Red Cross center, rolling bandages and boxing up care packages for the holidays. But this would be different. There was something more personal about this that appealed to her.

She turned to Izzy. "Where do I sign up?"

"That's the spirit!" Izzy said. "I have a sign-up sheet at my desk. Stop by at noon, then let's go out for a bite."

Before Lillian could agree, a young secretary stepped out of the elevator and ran up to Izzy.

"Miss Briggs! Come quick!" she said, breathlessly. "Mr. Rockwell has been looking for you everywhere. He wants the guest list for the dinner event on Thursday."

Izzy raised her eyebrows at Lillian. "We better make it 12:30."

Lillian nodded and watched as Izzy followed the young woman back to the elevator.

*

They entered their favorite café, not far from the office, and waited for a table to open.

"Good Lord," whispered Izzy, eyeing the white-haired waitress briskly clearing the table by the counter. "She looks like my grandmother. Even older, I'd say."

Lillian had noticed that the waitresses were getting older and older, though they seemed to have as much energy as the younger ones. She assumed the younger women were taking the higher paying jobs that were fast becoming available.

They slid into a booth, glanced at the menu, and quickly placed their orders. Then Izzy began talking about Archie, recounting how they had first met at a USO dance, how their romance had slowly blossomed, and that she was counting the hours until his arrival.

"I can't explain it, Lilly, but he's different from the other guys I've dated. I can't quite put my finger on it, but something about it just feels right." Then she shook out her napkin with a snap of authority. "And I am *not* going to let work interfere with our time together."

"No, you must spend any time you can with him," Lillian said. "Furloughs are too brief as they are."

"And now I have to *attend* the event on Thursday, as well as the gala on Saturday! But I told Rockwell – don't even *think* about asking me to stay late or give up my weekends for the next two weeks."

"He's become completely dependent on you, Izzy. I don't know what he would do without you."

"It didn't matter before, but now that Archie will be here I plan to leave at five o'clock on the dot," she said, tapping her finger on the table for emphasis. "I explained that to Rockwell, but I don't think he heard a word I said."

"I'm sure he'll understand," said Lillian, making room for the waitress to set down their plates.

"Rockwell – understand? Ha!" Izzy frowned at her anemic looking sandwich and picked it up. "I keep hoping he'll be drafted. He's not too old. Some time in the South Pacific would be good for him. Give him a little color." She bit into her sandwich and waved the image of Rockwell away.

"We only have two weeks together but we're going to make the most of it. I've got tickets to *Oklahoma!* and the Christmas Show at Rockefeller Center. I have every night all planned out."

Lillian smiled at Izzy's enthusiasm and her contagious zest for life. Izzy had endless energy and no matter what befell her, she took it on with gutsy determination.

"But here I am, going on and on about me. What about you? How about this Artists for Victory campaign? How do you see yourself participating?"

"I've been thinking about it all morning. I'll go to the orientation of course, but I've already got some ideas. I'm going to put together a few lesson plans, for different levels of experience."

As she explained what she had in mind, Lillian found herself growing more and more interested about this new turn of events.

They hurried back to the office, filled with excitement about the coming weeks. Lillian took a moment to look again at the Artists for Victory poster, happy that she was going to be a part of it.

She was just taking off her coat, when she noticed the envelope on her desk. Her heart contracted. Like everyone, she lived in fear of the dreaded telegram. But on opening the envelope, she saw that it was a message from the boys' school. Again. Her mouth tightened in anger as she read the note. Gabriel had not returned to school after lunch.

Though she felt less alarm than the first time she received such a message, her heart still quickened with worry. She let out a huff of exasperation. "Gabriel! What am I going to do with you?" She put her coat back on and grabbed her purse.

She could have understood if he wanted to play hooky with his best friend, Billy, with some purpose or adventure in mind. But no, Gabriel just liked to wander off on his own – at nine years old! For the third time this school year, she had to tell her boss that she had a family matter she must attend to.

Chapter 2

∽

Evening was settling in over the farmyard, and the outside activity that had enlivened the day, had moved into the farmhouse kitchen. Ed, the old farmhand, stood on the back porch, hesitant. He heard raised voices – female voices – and decided to wait a bit before delivering his news. He gazed out over the fields of corn stubble at the magnificent sunset. Bold streaks of orange and purple spanned the sky, edged with a rippling shimmer of pink. Beautiful and strong – just like the women inside the farmhouse, he thought with a shake of his head.

He'd worked on the farm for – what was it, now – must be over fifteen years, ever since he left the Water Works in town. Never thought he'd stay for so long. But after Kate's husband died – now there was a good man – he felt he had to lend a helping hand. Then just as he was about to retire for a second time, the war broke out, and one by one, Kate's sons left, leaving her alone with her two daughters. So he decided to stay on, and see them through the war.

Though if truth be told, he loved farm work. He'd grown up on a farm and was happy to spend some of his last years back in the country, closely connected to the earth. He loved the seasons, loved that first touch of green that dotted the fields in spring, the lush cornfields of summer, the sense of satisfaction at harvest time. He even loved the winter when the wide gray skies rested over the barren fields.

Glancing back at the kitchen door, he thought how he loved them all – Kate and her sons and daughters. He was fond of each and every one of them, but he couldn't help the soft spot he had for Ursula. Even as a curly-topped child, she had a way of winning people over with her wide-eyed wonder and her demand for answers – "But why? How? What would happen if…?"

He chuckled, remembering how she used to ride around with him on the tractor, how he helped her learn to ride a bike, how she and little Francy used to hold hands as they jumped from the hayloft. And how, after her father died, she had transferred much of the affection for her father onto him.

How quickly the years had passed. Now here she was, almost eighteen years old, and more headstrong than ever. Yet sweet as a summer day. A hard worker, and capable, yet he often caught her staring out at the sunsets, or wondering at the beauty of snow drifts, or listening to a strain of music on the radio with a hand pressed to her chest. There was a poet inside her, he often thought – though he doubted it would have the chance to come out now. If only she could have gone on to school, like she wanted. Well, there's still time, he thought. He gave another shake of his head at the memory of the little girl who used to romp around the farm. Ursula. Here she was, seventeen – a breathtaking beauty in overalls.

Now Jessica, he thought, giving a little nod. She had more chance for overall, everyday happiness. Was more practical, down to earth, did not set her expectations up there with the moon. And was dang pretty. But Ursula…

Ed rubbed his whiskers, and his tanned wrinkled face scrunched in worry. She had that kind of dark beauty that troubled the heart. He took off his hat, inspected the rim, and readjusted it on his head. Well, they're still young. It'll all work out, somehow – it always does.

He cocked his head and listened; all seemed quiet now. He went back to the door and raised his hand to give a soft rap. More loud voices. Nope. They never lasted long, these female storms, but best to wait, all the same. Though he loved them all, he had learned long ago to stay out of their arguments.

He walked to the edge of the porch and watched as the fire slowly left the sky and the streaks of orange settled into soft shades of pink. He looked out over the farmyard – all blue and gray in the growing dusk, except for the yellow light over the entrance to the barn and the light that poured from the farmhouse windows. His favorite time of day; it never failed to disappoint.

Kate turned up the burner on the stove and stirred the stew. She had been against getting a new stove, but her sons had surprised her with this one two years ago. Thank God they hadn't listened to her; with restrictions on metal there were no new appliances to be had now. If it weren't for her sons she would still be cooking on the old wood-burning stove. She tasted the stew, and added a pinch of salt, trying her best to ignore the stomping and pacing of her elder daughter.

Jessica, still in her school dress, carefully folded the calico napkins as she set the table. She raised her eyes now and then to observe the exchange between her sister and mother.

Ursula plopped down in a chair in her overalls, arms crossed, an angry fire burning in her eyes. The only adornment she allowed herself these days – and in Kate's eyes, evidence of her contrariness – were the amethyst drop earrings her family had given her after she was accepted into the women's college downstate. She wore them every day as a reminder that she *would* go to college. Some day. And though Ursula wouldn't admit it, she was just as hungry for a bit of beauty as was Jessica – perhaps even more so. In the middle of milking the cows, or feeding the chickens, or hauling firewood into the house, she would lightly touch the earrings – as a reminder of her dreams.

"I'm afraid it's the only way," said Kate, with more calm in her voice than in her heart.

"Over my dead body! I won't hear of it, Mother."

Kate was determined not to lose her temper. "And just how are we supposed to run the farm? Have you thought of that? When spring comes, what are we to do? Lose the farm because of your stubbornness?"

"Stubbornness!" Ursula jumped to her feet. "How can you say that? It would be disloyal to Francis to have some hateful *German* here in his place. I just can't do it. I won't do it!"

That tone of voice was the wrong one to use with Kate, who spun around, her face revealing a more fully-formed version of fire and determination than her daughter's. "This is *not* your farm. It belongs to the family, and you'll do what is right for us all. Your father broke his back making a go of this farm, and I will not lose it now!"

Ursula knew when she was in a losing battle. Her mother was always able to out-argue her, so she instinctively shifted to a different tactic. The goddess-of-vengeance attitude was softened with a pleading tone. "We have Ed, and we can hire high school boys for the summer. Until then, we can do the work ourselves. We'll manage."

"You and Jessica have been working too much as it is." Kate raised her hand at Ursula's protest. "I know, you can do more, and trust me, you're going to have to. But I can't have Jessica missing any more school. It's a wonder she hasn't fallen behind."

That argument quieted Ursula. She felt bad that Jessica's school time had been cut into over the past few months. "But now that the harvest is over – "

"No, Ursula. There's only so much that three women and one farmhand can do. Many of the farmers are using POWs. Are forced to do it. The Bloomfields have already started using them. There's more and more pressure to produce, to feed the troops. Have you thought about that? Your brothers need the food that farms like ours produce."

"And we have to help the poor British," said Jessica. She picked up her cat, Cotton, and began stroking her. "And the Russians. They're starving."

"Because the Germans are sinking our supply ships! That's my point," Ursula said, quickly reverting to her original position. "They're monsters! You've read the papers, heard the reports. They throw innocent people into horrible camps. They strafe the refugees, shoot down our paratroopers. The Nazis are despicable cowards! Nothing is too low for them. The last thing we need is one of them on our farm, on the pretext of helping with food production!"

"One? I'm hoping for several." Kate sliced the bread and then set it on the table, along with a slab of butter.

Ursula let out a groan of disbelief and sat down heavily in her chair.

Jessica gauged her sister's anger and tentatively added, "Shirley said her parents are happy with their POWs. They didn't see any other way to –"

"Well, Shirley hasn't lost a brother to the Nazis!" said Ursula.

Kate squeezed her eyes shut, and then gave the corn a brisk stir. She lifted the pan and emptied it into a bowl. "If any one of us got sick, then what? No. I can't risk it." She looked at the table, then out the window at the darkening night, seeing possible disaster everywhere. "The fences must be mended. The ditches need to be drained. The barn's falling apart. And come spring, how can we manage the planting with Paul gone?"

"What if they poison the well, or kill us in our sleep?" asked Ursula.

"They'll be taken back to camp at end of day, as you well know."

"Camp? It's hardly a camp. It's the Friedman's dairy farm that they've converted."

"It's a branch camp. They use whatever facility they can find. We're lucky to have one close by. Otherwise, we wouldn't be able to get the help we need."

Jessica tried to find neutral ground. "Ed said they used Friedman's Dairy in the Great War, as an induction center."

"For *our* men," countered Ursula. "Not to house a bunch of Nazi animals – "

"That's enough," said Kate. "It's settled. I've already put in a request."

A sullen silence followed. Jessica looked from her mother to her sister, wondering who would break first. They were equally stubborn, as far as she could tell.

Ursula's face twisted in despair. "Can you at least make sure they're Italian? Or even Japanese? I just can't stomach a Kraut."

"Shirley's dad said they don't allow the Japs to work," said Jessica.

"And no wonder! And the Germans are just as treacherous. At least request Italians."

Kate gave Ursula a look of reproach. "In case you haven't heard, Italy has surrendered. Is now with the Allies. We don't know what that will mean for the status of their POWs." She began to ladle the stew into three earthenware bowls. "Besides, I'll take whoever I can get."

"I wish Paul hadn't left," Jessica said wistfully, setting Cotton down.

"I'd enlist if they'd take me," said Ursula. "I'd love nothing better than to – to take on a few Nazis."

Kate smiled inside at Ursula's choice of words. She had expected her to say *shoot* or *kill*. For all Ursula's bluster, she couldn't bring herself to say anything stronger than *take on*.

Jessica ignored her sister's remark. "He could have stayed to help us run the farm. Who's going to help me gather berries? Who will help me with my honeybee project for the fair? I just know I could win the blue ribbon for my honey. If Shirley Bloomfield gets first place again for her peach preserves, I'll scream!"

"That's what you're worried about?" asked Kate. "We stand to lose the farm, and you're worried about the 4H?" She shook her head and rinsed the ladle under the tap.

"Paul is doing his duty," said Ursula. "He's doing his duty to Francis. He'd already tried to enlist twice before but they wouldn't take – " She stopped when Kate spun around.

"What? And you didn't tell me? I could have stopped him! What's wrong with you? Keeping secrets. Furious at the world. Letting that chip on your shoulder poison your life." Kate slapped her hand on the counter, taking the girls by surprise. "We all lost! Francis was my son!" she said, clenching her fist and hitting her chest. "And I've lost him."

Both girls were stunned into silence. They rarely saw their mother cry, and the possibility that she might now break filled them with fright.

Kate lifted her apron to her eyes. "But I will *not* lose the farm. Your brothers are coming back." She spun around again, wielding the ladle like a weapon. "Do you hear me? They're coming back."

"Yes, Mom," Jessica said, going to Kate and putting her arms around her.

That one of her children needed her, softened Kate back to calmness. She kissed Jessica's head and raised her chin. "Don't you worry. Your brothers will come back. And in the meantime, we'll manage the farm. Everything will be fine."

Jessica smiled up at her.

Kate gave her a squeeze, and glanced over at the hardened face of Ursula. With her eyes, Kate asked her to be on her side. "All right, my girls?" she gently asked.

Ursula forced a quick nod. But her arms remained crossed.

Kate shook out her apron, and hung it on the side of the broom closet. A knock came at the kitchen door, and their old farmhand stepped in.

"Come inside, Ed," said Kate. "Warm yourself with a bowl of stew."

He held his hat and shuffled around the door. "I'll be headin' home. Opal's got dinner waitin' for me. I just wanted to let you know – they'll be bringin' three POWs from the camp on Wednesday." His eyes darted to Ursula and back to Kate. "I'll see you all tomorrow." He put his hat on and backed out of the door.

Ursula abruptly scooted her chair back and stood. "Don't expect me to have *anything* to do with them!" She left the kitchen and ran upstairs.

Kate and Jessica heard stomping and door slamming, and soon the bathwater began to run.

Kate sat down at the large table, six seats empty. She looked up at the ceiling. "She's growing more and more stubborn. More and more bitter. I don't know what will become of her." She placed a saucer over the abandoned bowl of stew to keep it warm.

"She'll come around, Mom. She wasn't like this before Francis."

Jessica buttered a slice of bread, and considered how best to shift the conversation back to safe ground.

"Mom, how am I supposed to make my gingerbread house for the raffle without sugar?

We'll never have enough for all the things we need to bake."

Kate sighed. "We'll figure out a way, somehow."

"I'm going to the Martin farm tomorrow to see if I can trade some butter for some of their sugar coupons. It doesn't seem right that they get so many just because they have so many kids. They could never use them all."

"Everyone gets the same amount of ration coupons, per person," said Kate. "That's fair."

"Well I'm going to ask them before Sue Ellen does. Shirley says she's baking up a storm for the dance, trying to impress Joe Madden with her cooking. All she talks about is her famous apple strudel." Jessica exchanged a smile with her mother. "I know – it *is* delicious."

For the rest of the meal, Kate listened to Jessica talk about the Christmas dance in a few weeks and what she and her best friend, Shirley, were going to wear.

As they finished up, Kate took out a tray and set the bowl of stew and a few buttered slices of bread on it. "Bring this up to her."

Jessica took the tray upstairs, pushed open the bedroom door, and set the tray on top of the trunk. Ursula sat on the edge of her bed, towel drying her hair. Jessica saw that her eyes were red and swollen, but the anger had died out.

"Your hair smells of lavender," Jessica said with a smile. "It always reminds me of summer. It's been two years since we've made any lavender oil or soap. I'm going to make some next summer, come what may."

Ursula smiled at her sister. "The world is falling apart, and you're worried about lavender soap."

"We might as well smell nice while everything else is so awful. We need *some* beauty in our lives."

"You're right. In some odd way, that makes perfect sense."

"The same reason you wear your earrings all the time – even to bed."

"They help, somehow." Ursula's hand went up to her earrings. She looked at her reflection in the mirror, pulling her hair back to see the tiny glints coming off the faceted stones. "They're a reminder – "

"I know, I know – they're going with you to college. But still, there's nothing wrong with wanting to look pretty, in the meantime."

Ursula laughed. "There's not much point in that."

Jessica went into the adjoining room that she had fixed up as her own private bower, with yellow calico curtains and dried flowers. She claimed that Ursula's reading light kept her awake, but Ursula knew that she just liked the idea of having her own room.

Jessica washed up and soon returned to Ursula's room, wearing her nightgown with the embroidered yoke.

"Ursula," she said gently, "you're not the only one who loved Francis. We all loved him. And miss him. But you can't change what happened."

Ursula turned away and began brushing out her hair.

"I hate the Germans, too, Ursula. And I'm so afraid that one of the others will get hurt. But think of Mom. She lost Dad years ago – and now Francis. I don't think she could bear to lose the farm. It's her only connection to them all. It's what keeps her going – believing that the farm will be waiting for them when they return. We have to do whatever it takes to make sure that happens."

Ursula studied her little sister. "When did you become so wise?"

Jessica smiled at the rare compliment. "I think when Francis died. We all changed. I'll never forget Mom's face when the car brought the telegram. The way she stood on the porch, eyes fixed on that car. She knew. She knew. And she just stood there, waiting, tall and straight. But I saw her. She was shaking. Wondering which one it was. Mom loves us all, but Francis had a special place in her heart. In all our hearts."

Ursula took the towel and returned to the bathroom, not wanting to cry in front of her sister. The pain was still too raw. She couldn't bear to talk about Francis. She loved all her siblings, terribly – but Francis – well, he was the best human being that God had ever created.

Chapter 3

Lillian stopped by Mancetti's grocery store on her way home, and though her ration coupons didn't buy her much, she was able to put together a hasty dinner of meatloaf, potatoes, and canned peas. Since tomorrow was Meatless Tuesday, she was grateful for the small portion of ground beef she had been able to purchase. By adding some chopped vegetables and the dried bread she had been saving, she was able to concoct a meatloaf that the boys seemed to enjoy.

Over dinner, Lillian avoided looking at Gabriel – though seeing Tommy with his black eye now a pale green color, wasn't helping her aggravation at their behavior. She half-listened as Tommy went on about the holiday Boy Scouts' projects.

"We're going to start visiting the wounded soldiers in the hospitals. We made some Christmas decorations for them, and we're working on a play. Then we're going to bring them Christmas candy and sing carols."

Tommy leaned forward for another helping. "And I'm going to tell the soldiers that pretty soon *I'll* be old enough. Just a few more years, and I'll be a pilot and shoot down the Jerrys and Japs, blow them all to pieces."

Gabriel kept lifting his eyes, waiting for Lillian to look at him, waiting for a break in the wall of silence that excluded him.

"Nothing wrong with bombers," continued Tommy, "but *I'll* be flying a fighter plane. And there's only one plane for me – the P-38 Lightning." He used his hand to take off and dive, firing at the enemy. "I'll dive bomb those Japs and – "

"I said I was sorry, Mom!" Gabriel blurted out.

Only now did Lillian turn to him, still unsure how she wanted to handle him this time.

"You've already told me you were sorry. Twice before! And then you left school again." She stared at him, considering what to do. "I have half a mind not to let you go to Scouts."

Gabriel's eyes widened in alarm. "I have to go! I'm one of the Wise Men. It won't work with just two."

"We need him, Mom," said Tommy. "We're rehearsing for the hospital routine, and Gabriel can sing. You could take away his compass, or make him go to bed an hour early."

Gabriel looked over at Tommy, hoping he wouldn't continue with more suggestions.

"I won't do it again, Mom. I promise."

"This is the third time, Gabriel. Don't you understand that it's a dangerous thing to do? If you fell or got hurt or lost, I wouldn't even know."

"I know." Gabriel scrunched up his face, trying to figure out why he kept doing the things he meant not to. "I really didn't mean to do it. I just went out to the schoolyard at lunch to test my compass. I was going to go right back. Really, Mom. I was just checking the direction of the park. Billy said it was east, but I thought it must be southeast. And the next thing I knew, there I was, hiking in the park."

"For two hours!"

"But I didn't know it was that long."

She wanted to be angry with him, to scold him and mete out some kind of punishment to prevent him from leaving school again, but his sweet face always melted her. She knew that he was impressionable and had a hard time with routines and rules and restrictions. That dreamy side of him, that she knew he got from her, sometimes worried her.

"What were you doing for so long, Gabe?" asked Tommy.

"I told you. Exploring."

"It's Central Park," Tommy laughed. "Not the Amazon."

"But it's practice for when I go there. For when I climb Mount Kilimanjaro and explore the Gobi Desert. By then I'll know what to do – I'll be an expert!" His eyes filled with excitement remembering the afternoon's adventure. "I climbed those big rocks by the lake – "

"Gabriel!" said Lillian. "You were supposed to be in school. Do you want to flunk and have to repeat the fourth grade? You'll never get to the Amazon that way. Is that what you want?"

Gabriel had never considered that outcome. He blinked hard and swallowed. "No."

"Do you want me to lose my job? That's three times I had to leave work because of you. You cannot do this anymore." She waited for his acknowledgement. "Do you understand?"

He nodded, but Lillian remained unconvinced. Perhaps she was missing something. Perhaps there was some other reason he wandered away from school.

"You used to love school, Gabriel. What happened? Don't you like it anymore?"

"I still do. It's just that – "

"What?"

He looked around the table, thinking of how to explain. "Sometimes I just feel like running and climbing and discovering things on my own. There's a lot to learn outside, Mom."

Lillian let out a deep sigh. Then she placed her hand on Gabriel's arm. "That's true, Gabriel, but school is also important. Please don't run off like that again. It worries me too much." She leaned forward and rubbed his arm. "I'll take you to the park on the weekend, all right?"

Gabriel raised his face and smiled politely; she knew immediately that she hadn't said the right thing.

Lillian wondered if his life felt unsettled with the constant talk of war. Or did her fear and loneliness for Charles spill onto him? Charles had been called away so soon after they had married, and was away at sea for most of the time since then, that he barely had time to bond with the boys. Perhaps they felt his absence more than she realized. Izzy was right; they needed to be around family this time of year. Once again, she considered going upstate to her sister's. "Would you like to go to Annette's for Christmas?"

Gabriel's eyes grew round and he sat up in his chair. Lillian knew that she had said the right thing.

"Can we, please, please? We could go sledding and skating. And we could help Uncle Bernie find a Christmas tree. Can we really go?"

"Only if you promise – no more leaving school."

"Scout's honor!" said Gabriel, holding up three fingers in pledge. He leaned forward and took another helping of mashed potatoes.

Tommy now caught the excitement. "Will Danny be there? Oh man, we'll have so much fun. Can I bring the Spitfire plane I made and show him?"

"Of course you can," said Lillian. Perhaps that was all they needed, to be away from everything, to enjoy the coziness of a country Christmas. "We'll find a way for you and Gabriel to spend Christmas there. Even if I have to bring you there and come right back."

Tommy's head jerked up. "You mean – spend Christmas without you?"

Gabriel looked at Tommy, then back at Lillian. "We have to be together for Christmas, Mom. Won't Dad be home by then?"

"I don't think so, but I'm not sure." Lillian poured some gravy into the hole Gabriel had made in his mashed potatoes and then emptied the last of it onto Tommy's second helping. "I'm sure we'll get a letter soon."

Both boys sat silent, stunned at the possibility of not being all together for Christmas.

Lillian felt their eyes on her. "I'm thinking of joining an organization called Artists for Victory. On the nights that you boys have Scouts, I might work at one of the hospitals for our wounded servicemen. There's a meeting tomorrow night that I want to attend." She turned to Tommy. "Will you keep an eye on Gabriel and not leave the Scouts meeting?"

"Sure, Mom. That's what I always do. You know that. We'll just be down the street at Mickey's."

"And then I want you to go straight to Mrs. Kuntzman's. She's agreed to watch you until I get home."

Tommy was about to protest that he was almost thirteen years old, but he caught the warning look in Lillian's eyes and decided against it. Besides, nobody made better Christmas treats than their babysitter.

"What will you do at the hospital?" asked Gabriel.

"I'll find out more at the meeting. But I think I'll be giving drawing and painting lessons. Give the soldiers something to work at while they're recovering."

"Can I go with you sometime?" asked Gabriel.

Lillian smiled; he always surprised her. "Why would you want to go?"

He shrugged. "Just to see them. Talk to them. And I could help. I could hand out the pencils and paper, or rinse the paint brushes like I do for you."

Lillian watched Gabriel's sincere little face, and couldn't help thinking that he would make the soldiers happy.

"Yeah. I could go, too," added Tommy. "I could tell them that in four or five years I'll be able to shoot those stinkin' Jerrys and Japs. That would definitely make them happy."

Lillian closed her eyes against the possibility that Tommy and Gabriel would ever have to go to war. "I don't like all that talk about killing, Tommy."

"That's the only thing that will stop them from – "

"I know, but not from you. You have guns and fighting on your mind too much. Two black eyes in one month? Really, Tommy!"

They continued eating in silence, Lillian trying to think of who might be a good influence on Tommy.

"Why don't you invite Amy over to study this week?"

"Nah," said Tommy. "She's busy with her science club and Girl Scout stuff. Besides, she kind of talks a lot."

"Well, maybe that's because she has a lot to say," Lillian said, trying not to smile. She had noticed that whenever Amy was with Tommy, she did all the talking. Yet in spite of Tommy's comment, Lillian was sure that his sweet spot for Amy had not diminished.

Tommy lifted and dropped one shoulder. "I guess so."

"Could I go sometime, Mom?" asked Gabriel. "To the hospital?"

"We'll see," she said. "Let me go to the meeting tomorrow and see what it's all about." She glanced at the clock. "You better hurry to your Scouts meeting – Mickey and Billy will be wondering where you are."

The boys washed up and put on their Scout shirts and scarves. Lillian overheard Tommy telling Gabriel that in a few years he would have a real uniform – then Hitler, watch out!

The thought that the war might persist until the boys were old enough to fight filled her with dread. She constantly told herself that it couldn't possibly last that long.

She cleared the table and washed the dishes. After the boys left, she took up her needles and yarn, and curled up on the couch, listening to music on the radio. She usually spent part of her evenings knitting for Bundles for Bluejackets. Though she used to enjoy the time alone when the boys were at Scouts, lately she found herself waiting for it to be over. And the longer Charles was away, the worse the feeling seemed to get. She stared at the cold, empty grate of the fireplace, her hands and the ball of yarn resting on her lap. She had become a worrier this past year, imagining all sorts of horrible things. What it would be like to die an icy death. What it would be like to come home wounded. What if the war lasted years and years. What if Charles –

There were some thoughts she would not allow to take shape. She picked up her knitting, and cast on a few stitches. Teaching drawing to the soldiers. Now that was something new. It would help keep her mind off other things.

She tried to imagine herself in that role – and she drew a blank. What exactly would she teach? How many students would she have? Would she have to start at the beginning? And where was the beginning?

She set her knitting down and went to the bookshelves, looking for her old art books. She lifted the wedding picture of her and Charles, taken almost two years ago. Her heart swelled as she filled her gaze with his smiling face. He was so handsome. A longing rose up inside her, which she quickly suppressed. She had learned not to indulge in her yearning for Charles. She kissed the photograph, set it back on the shelf, and then looked for her art books.

There they were, on the bottom shelf. Dusty. She hadn't opened them in years. She brought them to the coffee table and browsed through the introductory chapters. Then she took out a notepad from the boy's school shelf, and began to make notes.

Chapter 4

On a chill gray morning, a pickup truck trundled up the dirt lane to Kate's farmhouse, carrying several German POWs and three guards. One of the guards was Otto Epstein, a veteran of WWI. Until recently, he ran his own farm not far from Kate's. But his rheumatism finally forced him to sell it and move into town. As a veteran, he wanted to do his part in this war and was pleased to find work at the recently established POW branch camp. He sat with the driver in the cab of the truck, rubbing his hands against the cold.

The truck pulled up to the machine shed where Kate, Jessica, and Ed were laying out the fencing materials. Jessica had convinced Kate to let her stay home from school so that she would be there for the arrival of the prisoners. Jessica had already missed several days at harvest time, and Kate didn't want her to miss any more. But she unreasonably felt that there would be strength in numbers today, and had given in to Jessica. Ursula stubbornly remained behind the shed, hammering away in a futile attempt to repair the tractor.

"Ursula!" Kate hollered out the back door. She waited a moment. Then she turned to Jessica. "Go tell her to come inside."

Kate walked out to the truck, a jolt of fear shooting through her. She realized how easily they could be overpowered by the Nazis.

With some difficulty, Otto climbed down from the truck, walked around to the back, and called out three names. The POWs jumped out, dressed in blue denim with the letters PW stamped on them. They lined up with their hands behind their backs, awaiting their orders.

Kate raised her head in goodbye to the driver, a man she recognized from the next town over. He noisily shifted gears and drove off to deliver more POWs to the neighboring farms.

"Mornin', Kate!" Otto said brightly, as if he had just dropped by for a friendly visit, and was not being followed by three prisoners of war. He carried the rifle issued from his WWI days.

Kate refrained from smiling and stepped up to give Otto a quick handshake, somewhat alarmed at the frailty of his gnarled hand. She quickly assessed the three POWs. One appeared to be in his mid-thirties, perhaps, the others in their early twenties. They all looked strong. Though she would never admit it to her daughters, she had been afraid that she would meet threatening eyes full of hatred and vengeance. She was relieved to see impassive, perhaps resigned, expressions.

Otto pushed his hat back and looked at the disappearing truck. "That's Zack Wells. He'll pick us up at four-thirty. I'll stick around, make sure everything goes smoothly." He walked over to Kate and spoke softly. "Course, there aren't enough of us for all the farms. Not sure if I'll always be able to stay the whole time. It will depend on how things work out, how many men you're going to need, how many guards they can find."

A flash of fear crossed her face, which she did her best to hide.

"Not to worry," said Otto. "These three come highly recommended by the camp coordinator. Has known all three of them for several months, says they're hard workers, can be counted on."

Good behavior in prison held little value for Kate.

"And they're available six days a week. Rather be earning a wage than sittin' inside a camp."

Otto waved the men over. "*Mach schnell*, lads. Over here. Meet the owner of the farm."

Kate looked at Otto with surprise. "Do they understand English?"

He shook his head. "No, but I mix it up with a little German and they seem to get the gist of things."

Kate noticed that although all three prisoners faced straight ahead, their eyes took in the empty fields, the wide open country that stretched for miles, the clump of trees that lined the pasture creek. A subtle shift occurred in their faces, something like a glimmer of happiness or the lifting of a burden. Were they happy to be out in the open? Did it remind them of home? Or were they seeing ample opportunity for escape?

When Kate nodded to them, they bowed their heads. And though they didn't smile, she thought she saw an expression of politeness in all of them. Or was she simply seeing what she wanted to see?

"Come inside here," said Kate to Otto. "Ed will show you what needs to be done."

Inside the machine shed, Jessica stood next to Ed, her hands fidgeting nervously at her sides. Her apprehension faded when she noticed her mother's confident stride, and Otto Epstein's familiar face.

Kate stood next to Jessica and addressed the POWs, speaking slowly and clearly, allowing for Otto to translate. "This is my daughter, Jessica. And this is our farmhand, Ed Barnaby." She looked around for Ursula, a flash of anger momentarily surfacing. "Just a moment."

Ed began to explain to Otto what they wanted done with the fencing, starting with the pasture and the south field. Otto, who had learned rudimentary German from his grandparents, then translated in a mix of the German from his youth, loudly-articulated English, and an abundance of large arm movements.

The sound of metal banging on metal came from the side of the shed, where Ursula was growing frustrated in her attempt to fix the tractor.

Kate walked to the back door. "Ursula!" she hollered, and waited for her daughter to look up.

Still holding the wrench in her hand, Ursula jumped down, strode past her mother, and walked into the machine shed, wearing an expression of disdain. She softened only to greet Otto, but avoided looking at the prisoners.

Kate followed her in and stepped up to Otto, waiting for him to introduce the three men.

"These are the POWs you requested. This here's Gustav – has his own farm over there in Germany," Otto said, waving his thumb towards the fields, as if it were somewhere nearby. "This is Karl – pretty quick to pick up English." The young man nodded and gave a wide smile. "And this is Friedrich. They all have farming experience."

Ursula kept her chin thrust out and barely acknowledged their existence – until the last of the POWs was introduced.

When Friedrich raised his eyes, Ursula stiffened. A look of dismay crossed her face for one brief moment, quickly replaced by contempt. She threw down the wrench and stormed out.

Kate stepped aside and took Otto by the arm. "I'm sorry, Otto. I'm afraid it's going to take her some time to get used to this. She's been dead set against it from the start."

Otto was about to ask a question, when understanding filled his face. "Francis. Of course. Can't blame her." He kicked the straw around with his boot. "I don't think you'll have any trouble with these three. But I'll try to keep them away from you all."

"Thank you, Otto. Go ahead and get started. I'll have lunch ready for you."

"No need. They have sandwiches."

"On this farm, everyone eats a hot meal for lunch." He was about to object but she put up her hand. "They'll get more work done that way." She looked around the shed and gestured to one corner. "It's warm enough for now. They can eat in here."

Kate and Jessica then left, leaving Otto and Ed to carry out the fencing instructions.

"That wasn't so bad," said Jessica.

"No, it wasn't." Kate was relieved that the first encounter was over, and that she didn't sense any menace coming from the prisoners. "Might as well get started with the washing," she said. "I'll be right in."

She turned around and watched Otto and Ed help the POWs hitch up the horse and cart, and load up the materials. One of the prisoners pointed to the tractor and said something to Otto. Otto waved his arms and made some answer, scratched his head, and pointed back to the horse and cart.

"Ursula!" Kate called out, seeing that her daughter was busying herself in the barn.

Ursula looked up, and walked over to her mother.

Kate waited until Ursula was standing in front of her, and then spoke softly but firmly. "I'll not tolerate that kind of behavior on this farm."

"I couldn't help it. It's an outrage!" In a lower voice, she added: "Otto Epstein – a guard? We all love him, but – *he's* what stands between us and the Nazis? God help us!"

"If you're so afraid we're in danger, then stop behaving like a petulant schoolgirl. Show some common sense, for God's sake, and a little more self-control."

Ursula colored at her mother's remark. That was not how she saw herself.

"They're here to work," said Kate. "We've wasted days chasing down the cows that get through that fence. Like it or not, we need their help."

Ursula remained silent, a swarm of conflicting emotions all over her. Then she went back inside the barn.

Kate returned to the farmhouse, thinking that she couldn't blame Ursula for her fear and aversion. She felt it as well. But if this was going to work, she would need her daughters' cooperation. Childish outbursts would get them nowhere. Could set them back.

Ursula occupied herself in the barn all morning, with an energy and efficiency that was unusual, even for her – milking, feeding, brushing, cleaning.

It was nearly lunchtime when Kate went out to get her. As she approached the barn, she saw Ursula put her hands to her lower back, and then wipe her forehead with her sleeve. Kate's heart filled with a piercing ache. She had so wanted Ursula to go to college, to learn and make a sweeter life for herself. With four strong sons, she had been sure it would happen. Then the war broke out. When Pearl Harbor was attacked, her eldest sons were whisked off to training, and everything changed. Jessica was happy with country life, but Ursula had wanted more. She had prepared diligently for the coming year at the women's college downstate, thrilled that her life was about to change. Now, instead of pursuing her beloved subjects of history and literature and French, there was her daughter, brushing the cow. How she wished that Ursula were now attending college. How she wished that her sons were still at home. How she wished that Francis had not been killed.

Kate stepped into the barn and spoke softly, her voice shaped by years of struggle and the abrasion of pain. "Come on in. Lunch is ready. Don't worry – you won't have to see them."

Ursula kept her eyes fixed on the ground as her mother spoke, and only lifted them once she was gone. She leaned her head onto the cow's neck. "What am I going to do, Clover?" she asked. "How can I be so unlucky?"

The docile cow blinked and swished its tail. Ursula slowly shook her head, and then straightened and addressed the cow with more energy. "I *must* be mistaken. It *can't* be the same man." She left the barn and went back to the house, stopping to wash her hands at the pump.

In the kitchen, Kate and Jessica piled up the plates with meatloaf, potatoes, and corn bread. Ed had taken two plates outside and came back in for the rest. "I'll eat out in the machine shed with them," he said. "Who knows, maybe I'll pick up a word or two of German."

Kate knew better than to object. It was Ed's way of making sure that all went well.

She was about to take out the last plate and a thermos of coffee, when Ursula suddenly reached for them and followed Ed out to the barn.

Jessica, with a breathy catch of surprise, looked over at her mother.

Kate stood with her mouth open. "I'll never understand her," she said. "She's contrary to the core."

Jessica shrugged. "I guess she's just showing us – and them – that she's not afraid."

A makeshift table had been set up in the shed using a plank resting on two bales of hay. The men sat on upturned crates, and jumped up when Ursula entered. Ed handed out two plates, and the POWs softly replied, "*Dankeschön.*"

Ursula took the last plate and handed it to the dark-haired man. Friedrich. He took the plate, but kept his eyes lowered. She stood before him, waiting for him to look up.

He slowly lifted his eyes to hers, with an expression that was almost apologetic.

Without a doubt, it was him. Dark, haunting eyes, a face that seethed with emotion without ever changing expression.

It was him. And she was sure that he recognized her. She closed her eyes and whipped around, vowing never to look on him again.

*

That night after supper, Kate sat at the kitchen table doing some mending. From the radio came a newscaster's scratchy voice, clipped and taut as he relayed the evening news.

Ursula sat across from her mother, examining a pair of old overalls, carefully cutting out the parts that were not threadbare. Then she separated them into sizes – some for patching, others that could be used for quilts. When the news program concluded, and music began to fill the air, Ursula saw the same release of tension in her mother that she also felt.

Jessica had spread out her homework on the table, but was now on the phone with her friend Shirley.

Ursula had her ear tuned to the conversation. Jessica had called Shirley to discuss their history assignment, but she was soon comparing notes about their POWs: Did they feel safe? What were they like? How many? What was their behavior like?

Then she heard Jessica say that one of theirs was older and seemed nice and had a farm of his own. And that the other two were young and handsome. "Especially the one with dark hair."

Ursula shot her a look, and Jessica quickly added, "Too bad they're nasty Krauts. And they don't speak a word of English."

Kate observed Ursula's close attention to Jessica's conversation and wondered at her silence. Ursula's anger was gone, replaced by something more akin to sadness. Though her elder daughter was so much like herself, there were parts of Ursula that she could never quite fathom.

Jessica finished her call and sat back at the table, flipping through her notebook.

"Shirley says they've had the same five POWs for two weeks now, and they've started laying out the new barn. She said her dad wouldn't be surprised if they had it finished by Christmas. He's requesting the same men to help him with the planting in the spring."

"Makes sense," said Kate, biting off a thread.

Ursula's head snapped up. "I think we should try to find different ones. I don't like this group." Ursula knew her assertion sounded weak, but she hadn't been able to think of a legitimate reason for requesting different men.

"They seem all right to me," said Kate. "Ed said he and Otto found them easy to work with."

Ursula stared at the floor, concern clouding her face.

Kate noticed it, but kept her eyes on her sewing. "In one day, they finished mending the fence in the pasture," she said, in justification of her decision to use the POWs. "Otto said once he's confirmed that we can have them for a few weeks, they can get started on repairing the barn."

"Ed said they're hard workers," Jessica added timidly, afraid of rousing her sister's anger. "He thinks they like farm work."

"As opposed to killing people?" asked Ursula.

Kate ignored her comment. "We're lucky Otto speaks a little German."

The three of them sat in silence for several minutes, as was their habit. Then Jessica continued with her train of thought.

"Shirley said one of theirs has the same name as a boy who rides the bus with us – Kurt Reinhardt – and that he even kind of looks like him, with the same white-blond hair."

Kate considered this and nodded. "I wouldn't be surprised if they're related. This area was largely settled by Germans, along with Italians and Irish. Some Poles and Slavs." She held the needle away as she began to thread it. "I've heard that some of the prisoners have close relatives here that visit them at the camps."

"Otto said they get three good meals a day," said Jessica, "and that they play music and have sports teams and – "

Ursula set her sewing down, appalled. "Such a nice, comfortable life – while our men are being shot at and killed?"

"Think about it, Ursula," said Kate. "If word gets back to Germany about how well we treat our POWs, perhaps it will help our boys over there."

"I doubt it," Ursula answered with a huff of contempt.

A few more minutes passed in silence. Then Jessica, biting the eraser on the pencil, looked up at her mother.

"Mom?" she said softly.

"Hmm?" Kate asked, briefly glancing up from her sewing.

"I was all ready to hate them. I really was. But it's hard to do when they look like our neighbors. When they look like us."

Ursula could listen to no more. "Listen to you. They're brutal Nazis! They're killing our men. Doing horrible things to the Poles and Jews. You've read the papers, seen the newsreels. Don't be fooled by their appearance. They're *nothing* like us. They're cold-blooded murderers. Never forget that."

She stuffed the remnants of the overalls into the rag basket, and then stood stiffly, sore from overdoing her chores.

"You look all done in, Ursula," said Kate. "Why don't you go soak in a hot bath? It's been a long day."

Ursula went upstairs and ran the bath water, letting her clothes drop heavily to the linoleum floor. She looked at her reflection in the mirror, pushing aside her hair. She did look done in.

She touched the amethyst earrings. It had been so long since she felt pretty, since she had worn a dress, since she had gone to a dance. Everything now was bleak and grim. Her brothers, and most of the town boys, were gone. Everyone was having a hard time, having to adapt to all the changes. For the most part, she didn't mind. She loved the farm, loved the fields at sunset, had even learned to love the backbreaking work. It kept her mind focused, prevented it from filling with daydreams. Foolish dreams of college and travel, of seeing the beautiful capitals of Europe. She wondered if those cities would even still be standing after this nightmarish war was over.

The steam gradually blurred her reflection – just as her dreams had blurred and faded, she thought. No matter. There wasn't time for girlish daydreams. Her mother was right; she had behaved childishly today. Work needed to be done, and she would do it. The best thing was to keep busy and not think about anything too much.

And yet there was such a void. A black ugly void created by the war, created by Francis's death, and the unknown. Would her brothers come back? Would they win? Or would the Germans bomb them and take over, as they had done throughout Europe? A vision of smoky rubble, tattered figures, and scorched farmland filled her mind.

No. Germany would not win the war. The Japanese would not win. They were being pushed back. This is our war now, she thought, and we will win. If the armed services were made up of men like her brothers, then victory was sure.

Ursula tested the water, and added a few drops of lavender oil. Then she lit a candle and turned off the overhead light. The candlelight and the faint scent of flowers helped to soften her world. She eased herself into the water.

From downstairs came the voices of her mother and sister, Jessica finding something to giggle about. Ursula was glad to have some time alone, to sort out her thoughts.

The face of the German prisoner had filled her mind all day, though she had tried to rid herself of it. Friedrich. It would have been better if he had remained nameless. She slowly shook her head in disbelief at the earlier memory of him – one that had haunted her for almost two months now.

The memory of that day remained fresh and clear in the front of her mind, perhaps from going over it so many times. It had been in October. They had driven to town, giving Shirley and her mother a lift. While Kate and Mrs. Bloomfield ran their errands, Jessica and Shirley shopped for fabric, dragging Ursula along with them to help them choose. When they finished, they waited on the main street outside the drug store, where they all planned to meet.

Ursula had idly observed the traffic. With gas rationing there was less of it, and yet the roads were busy enough with people going about their business. Jessica and Shirley chatted about the harvest dance, and giggled over stories from school, while Ursula listened to Mrs. Kryzinsky, who stopped by to say hello. Soon the older woman was talking about the rationing, then about what was happening "back in old country," her memories of Poland, and what she feared it must look like now. The weight of war was everywhere.

Ursula had turned her gaze to the town square where the tall trees released their leaves to the sunlight – dazzling maples in orange and red, yellowing birch, their leaves falling slowly, like feathers. Then a sudden gust shook the trees and filled the air with shimmering leaves! Ursula felt a rush of longing and hungered for the beauty of the day. She inhaled the scent of dry leaves swirling about, and took in the rustle of wind in the high trees, the flock of dark birds that rose with the gust and scattered among the branches. Then calm once again suffused the day. She closed her eyes and let the sun's rays warm her, wondering at her sad tranquility. It was not the raw pain that had consumed her since Francis's death, but a distanced melancholy. A sad resignation at the ways of the world and her small place in it – set against the aching loveliness of the October day. It didn't seem right that she should feel such calm while the world ravaged on in pain and suffering. How could the world be filled with such horror, alongside such beauty?

An unmarked bus had slowly pulled up to the stop sign. Ursula hadn't given it much attention, until she saw that all the windows were full of soldiers. She had never seen such sad looking men, and her heart went out to them. One face stood out from all the rest, arresting her by its sad beauty. A young man with soulful eyes gazed out the window, his mind seemingly far away. He was suntanned, with chiseled features that seemed at odds with the softness in his eyes. He had looked down and met her gaze – and something happened inside her. Ursula was never one to flirt or show undue interest in a boy, but this face had struck some deep chord in her and she kept her eyes on his.

Neither of them turned away, but drank deeply from the other. Some agreed-upon door had opened, allowing them easy passage into one another.

I could love this man, Ursula had surprised herself with thinking. In her mind, she placed her hand on his cheek, and brought his face close to hers.

When a second bus squealed to a stop behind the first, Jessica and Shirley turned around and saw the busloads of young men. The girls began waving to them energetically, all smiles and friendliness.

In an instant, the sad faces brightened, the men sat up and waved back – except for Ursula's soldier. He continued to look at her with no change in his handsome face.

"What youse girls giggling at? Who youse make eyes at?" Mrs. Kryzinsky turned around to see for herself – and her face contorted with hatred. She swatted down the girls' arms and spat on the ground. "They're Germans, you stupid girls! Prisoners who deserve to be shot!" She continued in Polish, growing increasingly irate.

Jessica and Shirley froze, alarmed at their mistake.

The prisoners' faces instantly became, if possible, even sadder. A shadow of pain filled the young man's face, but he did not turn his eyes away.

Ursula's face had shown stunned disbelief – and then, anger. Outrage.

Then the buses drove on, through the town, and away.

A crowd slowly gathered, shocked that POWs were being driven through their town. Up until that moment, the enemy was far away, across the States, beyond an ocean. It seemed too risky to bring them here, drive them through town, and dump them off in the heartland. What was going on?

The local newspaperman provided the scant information he had.

"Those are Germany's elite – the Afrika Corps. Uncle Sam's been shipping prisoners over here ever since Rommel was defeated. England has no more room to house them. It's all hush-hush. The ships that bring thousands of our men to the docks of Europe, fill up with POWs for the return trip home. We've started to use them to help close the labor gap."

One old-timer took off his hat and scratched his head. "All backwards, to my way of thinking. And yet we're short on workers."

"Even with the women and old men working," added Mrs. Bloomfield. "I read they're even using the blind and crippled. But Nazis in our backyard? Good heavens!"

They watched the buses head north in the distance.

"We don't want them here!" the town grocer yelled.

"Lock your doors," added another.

"Keep 'em over there in Europe somewhere."

Another man stepped up. "Too late for that. My brother-in-law in Missoura says they got them there. And in Arkansas and Texas. Heard Texas woulda lost their entire cotton crop without their help. They send them to military camps, or sometimes tent cities until prison camps can be built."

The owner of the feed store had been listening and nodded his head. "The wife's got an uncle working up there at Camp Grant, near Rockford. Says the ones coming in are hardcore Nazis, captured in North Africa. And they're none too happy about it. Says they're just bidin' their time – waitin' for Hitler to make his way here. And they'll be sittin' pretty, all rested and fattened up – on *our* food."

"And ready to get back at their captors," added the grocer.

Mrs. Bloomfield raised her chin, indignantly. "Except for that they're losing. They just don't know it yet."

There was a lot of head shaking, and hands clasped at coat collars, as if against the cold.

Ursula had listened in fear and anger – and a nauseating sense of shame that she had looked kindly at the enemy. She had gazed at a Nazi with love.

The candle sputtered and flickered, and Ursula put her face in her hands at the memory. She finished her bath, and quickly dried herself. Then she put on her blue flannel nightgown, and sat on the edge of her bed where she began to towel dry her hair.

But after a few moments, she dropped the towel onto her lap. *And now here he is on our farm!* She groaned in despair.

She had known immediately that it was the same man. She'd had the same piercing feeling when he looked at her today. But she tried to convince herself that the coincidence was too great, that the buses had surely driven on to Chicago, taking him far away. So she had taken the lunch plate out to him, to put her fears to rest. But there was no doubt. It was him.

Ursula went to the window and looked out into the darkness. She hated him – for stealing a part of her unknowingly, for turning her, however briefly, into a traitor.

The more she thought of him, the more she hated him. She tightened her arms around herself, revulsion and scorn filling her face. For all she knew, he was the German who had killed her brother.

Chapter 5

Lillian waited outside the main office of Rockwell Publishing, not wanting to interfere with the tug-of-war between Izzy and Rockwell. Izzy was putting on her coat and nodding patiently to Rockwell as she signed for a late day delivery.

Rockwell waved around a stack of papers in front of her. "And these lists must be finished by Friday. Are you listening to me, Miss Briggs? Izzy! Did you hear what I said?"

Izzy smiled sweetly while she buttoned her coat. "Every word. And as I assured you earlier, it's all under control." She glanced at the clock. "Ah. It's five-fifteen, and I'm late. Goodnight, Mr. Rockwell."

Izzy came out into the hall, pressing down her splayed hands softly, as if silencing anyone who might wake the fussy child she just put to sleep.

They hurried to the elevator that was just opening. "Good Lord! That man tries my patience." She breathed a loud sigh of relief when the elevator doors closed behind them.

"Thought I'd wait and walk with you a few blocks," said Lillian. "I have to take the crosstown bus."

"So, tonight's your first class. Are you nervous?"

"A little," Lillian admitted.

"You'll be fine," Izzy said, pulling on her gloves.

"I don't know. I've never taught drawing before – or anything, for that matter. I hope they don't think I'm a phony."

"They're lucky to have you. Besides, it's an informal thing. The guys'll be happy for the company, and it'll help take their minds off being in a hospital."

"I'm sure you're right," Lillian responded, though the worry didn't leave her face. They exited the elevator, made their way through the crowded lobby, and then walked out onto the busy avenue. "And what are you and Archie doing tonight?"

Izzy's face flushed with pleasure. "We're going to my favorite little restaurant on Bleecker Street, and then out dancing." Izzy caught Lillian's look of surprise. "What?"

Lillian almost asked if it was the place she and Red used to frequent, but decided against it. "Nothing."

"Don't worry about tonight. I want to hear all about it tomorrow. And you're sure about next Saturday?"

"Yes. Tommy and Gabriel have a Boy Scouts outing. They've been working on a badge related to the war effort – studying maps, learning to identify planes, eating meals similar to K-ration. Without the cigarettes, of course. And next Saturday they'll be putting on a Christmas show for the GIs at a hospital." Lillian turned to Izzy. "Gosh!"

"What is it?"

"I can't remember the last time the boys and I were apart for the night."

"High time then. It'll be good for you to have a night out. And I can't wait for you to meet Archie." Izzy caught site of her bus just pulling up across the street. She gave Lillian a quick hug goodbye. "Five bucks says I can catch it!"

Lillian smiled as Izzy ran to catch her bus. She hadn't seen Izzy this happy for a long time. Not since she and Red were a couple. Lillian couldn't help wondering if Izzy was trying to recreate a better time in her life – when she and Red were young and in love with their future bright before them.

Then she realized that everyone had that tendency, including herself. Tonight she felt all the excitement of going to her introductory art class when she first moved to New York City. She had been so hopeful and excited, and had dreamed of having a small studio someday where she could devote herself to painting and drawing. Now she was the instructor. The knot in her stomach tightened as she boarded the crosstown bus.

She moved to the back of the crowded bus and found a seat. Then she opened her purse and took out the last letter from Charles. The envelope was worn from so many readings. Though she knew the letter by heart, she wanted to look at his handwriting, to read the lines about his love for her: *Every night I look out across the black ocean and know that you are there. The thought of you, of holding you against me again, is what gets me through the darkest times. All my love, until we're together again.*

Lillian tucked the letter back into her purse and stared out at the bustle of the city. But her mind stayed with Charles. She wondered how the war would change him.

She couldn't help but think about Izzy and Red; they had been so close. She was still shocked to think that Red had broken off their engagement and married his nurse in England. Red had been wild about Izzy. Could it happen to her and Charles? She pressed her eyes closed, telling herself that all she cared about was his safety. If he came home, if he lived through the war, nothing else mattered.

She sat up and glanced through the art supply bag on her lap. Her stomach fluttered a little as she stepped off the bus and walked to the hospital.

Mrs. Coppel, the hospital coordinator for Artists for Victory, greeted Lillian outside the recreation room on the third floor.

"Good evening, Mrs. Drooms. And once again, thank you for agreeing to help out. I know the Christmas season is a particularly busy time – but it's also the time when our wounded men need a little extra cheering on."

"I'm happy to be here. I just hope I don't disappoint them."

"Nonsense. They'll be delighted." She gestured to the instructor inside who was just making her final remarks. "As soon as she finishes, I'll introduce you to the men. Then you'll be on your own."

Lillian peered inside the room at the patients. A small group – very small – was participating in the demonstration on painting Russian eggs. The instructor had a kind, grandmotherly air about her, and encouraged three or four men to follow her instructions. Lillian was impressed with her degree of ease and confidence.

"Next week I'll bring in some hollowed-out egg shells and we'll give it a try. Well now, I see that our time is up for tonight." She gathered her supplies, and patted the men on their arms as she looked at their designs before leaving. "At the rate you're progressing, you should all have a beautiful egg or two to present to your loved ones for Christmas."

The coordinator exchanged a few words with the Russian lady as she left, while Lillian more closely observed the patients scattered about the room. A group of GIs played cards, others gathered around the radio. Some flipped through worn issues of *Yank* magazine, and a few others sat reading books or writing letters. A desultory attitude pervaded the group, and Lillian was suddenly afraid that she was not up to the task.

"You're on," said Mrs. Coppel with a smile.

Lillian's heart jumped and she followed her into the room. She took off her hat and coat and set them on the chair. A quick glance around revealed that most of the men hadn't even noticed the change of instructors.

Mrs. Coppel addressed the room in a loud voice. "Good evening, men. Tonight we're starting a new class. This is Mrs. Lillian Drooms. She'll be teaching Introduction to Drawing. There are tablets and pencils for anyone who's interested. Just come up and help yourself."

She then took a piece of chalk from the blackboard and handed it to Lillian. "Go ahead and write your name and the title of the class. I'll stop by in an hour." She gave Lillian an encouraging smile and left the room.

Lillian tried to emulate the coordinator's brisk manner as she wrote her name and class title on the blackboard.

A loud whistle came from one of the men playing cards, causing most of the others to turn their attention to Lillian. Slowly the rows of chairs in front filled, and several men pushed their wheelchairs closer to take a look. A low buzz of talking and laughter soon rose from the room.

The blood rushed to Lillian's face and she completely forgot her lesson plan. She glanced at the chalk board and saw that her writing slanted up at a sharp angle – sure sign of an amateur instructor. She wanted to erase it, but decided not to draw attention to it.

"Good evening, gentlemen. Please take your seats so we can get started." Lillian realized that her voice hadn't carried over the increasing hubbub. No one was taking her seriously.

"Please. Take your seats so – "

The rowdiness was steadily growing. One GI with a cane hobbled up to Lillian and held out his hand. "Nice to meet you."

Lillian shook his hand distractedly, and then heard a comment from the back of the room about drawing nudes, followed by howls of laughter. She realized that she was fast losing control of the situation. Her temper suddenly flared and she clapped twice loudly.

"That's enough, boys!" she yelled.

Then she blushed deeper, realizing that she was treating them just as she would Tommy and

Gabriel. But the tinge of anger in her voice had an effect; the group quieted.

"All right. Let's get started."

Though there was still some sniggering and elbowing, Lillian ignored it and began to teach.

"Perhaps we can start with introductions. For those of you who are interested in drawing lessons, why don't you tell me your names and whether you've had any experience – "

"You mean with drawing?" came a voice from the back, and the laughter started up again.

"Yes, with drawing. And those of you not interested in learning, can go back to what you were doing."

None of the men got up. A few leaned forward, as if awaiting some fun.

Lillian nervously picked up her lesson plan, looked at it, and then set it back down. She leaned forward on the table.

"I'm afraid I'm rather new at this. I've never formally taught a class before, but I work as an illustrator and have some experience. So perhaps we can learn from each other."

A few men kept the teasing alive with more under-the-breath comments: "Can I get a private lesson?" and "I'd love to teach you some things I know."

Part of Lillian wanted to collect her materials and storm out of the room.

Then the man with the cane, who she assumed was the ringleader, suddenly smacked the table with the end of his cane, causing Lillian to jump.

"Can it!" he hollered. "Let the lady do what she came here to do. If you want to learn how to draw, stick around. The rest of you – scram. Go on, beat it!" He turned to Lillian and gave a small bow. "Sergeant Remling – at your service."

Most of the men remained, coming up to the table to get tablets and pencils. A few trickled off and went back to their card game. They kept turning their heads, not wanting to miss out on any developments.

Lillian nodded a brief thanks to the sergeant.

"Okay, let's begin." She turned to a young man sitting at the end of the front row. "Why don't you start with your name?"

He politely gave his name. And then one by one, the others introduced themselves, giving Lillian time to regain her composure. Most of the men went by their nicknames: Alabama, Bushwick, Mack, Lefty, Bull, Memphis, Curly. She tried to remember as many of them as she could. A glance at the clock showed that fifteen minutes had already passed and she hadn't taught them anything.

A few of the younger men were clearly there for fun. One asked, "Now your turn, teacher. Tell us *all* about yourself."

"For now, my name will have to suffice. We're running out of time. Why don't we get started with a basic exercise? Turn to the person next to you and draw a brief sketch. After five minutes, you'll switch." She could sense hesitation and coaxed the men to give it a try. "Don't worry about what it looks like. I promise you'll get better. It's just a matter of practice."

Sergeant Remling had taken a seat in the front. "You're closest to me. Mind if I draw you?"

"Not at all." She faced him and smiled.

She heard a whistle and some laughter from a few of his friends. "Watch out for Rembrandt," one of them called out.

"Rembrandt?" she asked, addressing the sergeant.

"Remmy. Rembrandt. Dutch. I got a lot of nicknames," he said with a wink. "Rembrandt – that's the guys making fun of me on account of my appreciation for the finer things in life. Art and music. Fine wine. Beautiful women."

Lillian disregarded his flirtatious words and glanced at the clock. "All right. You have ten minutes to make your sketches. Don't judge your work. Just try to depict what you see."

One patient moved to the front and jerked his thumb back at his friend. "I'll be damned if I'm gonna to draw his ugly mug. Mind if I draw you?"

He didn't wait for Lillian's response, and started to sketch her.

Then another came forward. Lillian was losing control of the group again.

"All right. That's enough." She put her hand up at a few others who were about to move closer to her. "It doesn't matter who you draw. It's about training your eye." She waited for the hand to land on twelve. "Okay – begin."

She sat still since a few men were drawing her, but she kept encouraging the more serious ones. "Try to keep your hand fluid, the pencil moving."

From the back row, one GI repeated her words to the man beside him, putting a different spin on them. "Keep your hand fluid, Mack," he said, eliciting a few guffaws.

Lillian was about to reprimand them, but when she looked over at them, they smiled sweetly, all politeness. She hid the fact that she was rattled, and tried to build on the courtesy that most of the men showed her.

She was appalled to find that, to each other, they were astonishingly abrasive. "Keep still, Crip, and stop your hacking!" one man said to the patient he was trying to draw.

Another looked over at the sketch a one-armed man was attempting: "Jeez! And that's your good hand? Thank God it was the other arm you lost."

Others simply snorted in amusement at the various results.

After ten minutes she called time. "Okay, let's take a look at your first efforts." She walked around the room and made a few comments, encouraging some, offering suggestions to others.

When she came to Sergeant Remling, however, he became self-conscious, not wanting to show his drawing.

Lillian insisted. "This is just a simple assessment so I know where to begin. How else am I supposed to help you?"

He slowly handed over his sketch, keeping his eyes down.

Lillian almost burst into laughter. Could he be serious? His rendition of her was not much better than a child's drawing – round head, curly scribble hair. She placed her hand over her mouth, realizing that this was the best he could do.

Remling put on an exaggerated wounded expression. "Aww, you're not laughing at me, are you, Teach?"

"No. Of course not. This is an introductory class. You'll improve. You'll see." She was glad he was being good-natured about it. Though when she looked at the rest of the drawings, most were not much better.

"I want you to keep your drawings so that we have something to compare your progress against." She glanced at the clock. "Let me use the rest of our time to go over some basics." She spoke for another fifteen minutes and gave a few examples on the chalkboard, but she was unsure whether she was getting through to the men.

At the end of class, she gave two assignments: a still life and another portrait sketch. Several of the men delayed her with questions about drawing and about herself. She answered a few general questions, and, taking her coat and hat, she backed out of the room.

As she left, she heard a burst of laughter. One of the men had snatched up Sergeant Remling's drawing and was holding it high, to the immense entertainment of the others. No one was laughing harder than Remling himself.

Lillian was about to step back in and say something about respecting each other's efforts, but she sensed that there was a deeper dynamic at work, one that she didn't quite yet understand. A certain toughness mixed with dark humor. During class she had overheard several joking remarks about each other's wounds or handicaps, but each time they were met with a chorus of laughter. She closed the door behind her.

"Sorry I'm late!" said Mrs. Coppel, rushing up to Lillian. "Well – how did it go?"

"I – I'm not sure," answered Lillian, looking back through the glass door at the patients. "I'm not sure how much they learned."

The coordinator gave an easy chuckle as she glanced inside. "At least they're enjoying themselves. That's an improvement in itself."

Lillian gave a start when she saw one of the men, the one called Bull, grab a patient's wheelchair and tip it backwards, almost to the floor. The patient hollered in anger, swinging his arms behind him – and then started laughing.

Mrs. Coppel recognized Lillian's dismay. "You *will* be coming back, won't you?"

"Of course," smiled Lillian. "And the next time, I'll be better prepared. I was caught a bit off guard today."

"Splendid! Perhaps next time you could stop by the ward upstairs and talk to a few patients unable to leave their beds. Some of them are quite dejected, but have expressed an interest in the drawing class."

"I'd be delighted."

"It would be much appreciated. Not everyone makes the time for individual cases. It will surely do them good. I strongly believe in the healing properties of art, don't you?"

"Yes, indeed," agreed Lillian. Though she wondered how much healing she'd be able to bring about with this particular group.

Chapter 6

❧

Despite Otto's assurances that the POWs would be no trouble, Kate and Ed maintained a watchful eye and kept them away from the house. But after a week of working with them, Kate was beginning to come to the same conclusion as Otto. Yes, they were the enemy, or at least their country was, but they were hard-working, decent men.

They were friendly and courteous, appreciative of her cooking, and they seemed to take great pleasure in the outdoors. They even seemed eager to please. Of course, it could all be a ruse, thought Kate. She tried to keep a clear vision and constantly reminded herself that they were German soldiers. Yet her instincts told her that these were good men. And she couldn't deny the results they were bringing about on the farm. The fences in the pasture and south field were mended, and to her delight, the tractor was now running and in full use, after being in disrepair for weeks.

On the second day, she had come out onto the porch on hearing the sound of the tractor. There was Otto, driving the tractor in wide circles, a proud smile spread across his face at Kate's surprise.

Ed had laughed and stepped up onto the porch. "That fella Friedrich asked if he could try to fix it. Used his lunch hour to give it a go. Seems he has some mechanical ability. Runs like new."

They all watched as Otto drove the tractor to the barn. Kate caught Friedrich's eye and nodded her thanks.

A faint softening filled his handsome face, and he turned his eyes to Ursula.

She had stepped onto the porch with a dish towel in hand. "He's probably good with explosives, too." And she stepped back inside.

Ed saw the frustration in Kate's face. "We'll take it down to the creek and chop up those fallen trees I've been wantin' to get to. We can get a cord of wood out of them – maybe two." He looked up at the sky. "The weather's sure to change soon enough." Ed took off his hat and swatted it with his hand, smoothed his hair, and put his hat back on. He then joined the men outside the barn. Gustav and Friedrich hitched a large cart to the tractor, and soon they all drove off towards the creek.

Since that day, she and Ursula increasingly argued about the prisoners. Kate understood Ursula's anger, but it was getting in the way of running the farm. There was enough to worry about without Ursula constantly finding fault, especially with Friedrich. Ursula targeted him with most of her contempt. He seemed to want to help, and Ursula resented it.

Yesterday Kate noticed that Friedrich used his lunch break to finish chopping and stacking the branches that Ursula had started on. Earlier, he had watched as Ursula worked, pushing her hair off her forehead, rubbing her sore palms. It seemed to pain him. Though Ursula strode around as if she were strong, she was small-boned and most of her strength came from sheer determination. When Ursula came back outside after lunch, she saw the neatly stacked branches, glanced towards the POWs, and went back inside, slamming the door behind her.

Kate remained torn. She wanted to keep a distance from the prisoners, yet she was grateful for their hard work. And the nature of farm life was such that some interaction must take place. The truth was she liked them all, and appreciated their mild, respectful manner. In her mother's heart, she believed that mothers were the same the world over. Perhaps one day, some German mother might show a kindness to one of her sons.

As they'd grown used to each other, Kate relaxed her hold on the reins and allowed for simple, human interaction. Otto had filled her in on the scant information he had learned about the prisoners.

The oldest, Gustav, was married and liked to talk about his family. He had two little boys that he missed terribly and the best of wives. He was sick of fighting and only wanted to get back to his farm.

The youngest, Karl, had seen just two weeks of duty before being captured – and was apparently relieved by it. He was proud of the little English he knew and was always trying to catch a new word or phrase.

Friedrich didn't fit the stereotype of Rommel's men either. He had been part of the Signal Corps and hadn't seen much fighting. His main duty was the repair of radios and equipment. Otto said Friedrich was a hard nut to crack and that he kept to himself for the most part, though he got along well with the others.

Kate stood on the porch. She rubbed her arms and pulled her coat close. She looked at the mottled gray sky and took a deep breath, trying to calm herself; she and Ursula had just argued again. With the colder weather, Kate had told Ed to bring the prisoners and Otto inside to eat, which set Ursula off. Both mother and daughter had stormed out of the house – Kate to the front porch, Ursula to the back of the house.

Kate raised her face to the sky again and flexed her fingers. Snow was on the way; she could feel it in her joints. The extra wood the prisoners had cut gave her a degree of comfort against the coming winter – and there were more trees to be felled, more wood to be chopped. She gave a firm nod, as if in support of her argument. Ursula's room would be warmer this winter. Did she think of that? And Ursula would have more hot water to soak in the tub, as she was so fond of doing. Had she considered that? A hot meal in a warm kitchen was the only decent thing to do.

And yet – she still had doubts that she was doing the right thing in having them on the farm at all, let alone in her kitchen. She needed their help, but she also felt a sense of betrayal. The reports from the front filled her with terror. There was still a knot in her stomach from hearing Edward R. Murrow's recent "orchestrated hell" report. Her own son, Eugene, was in just such a plane, flying somewhere over Europe – flak exploding all around him, enemy planes swooping down, smoky ruins below.

Of course she understood Ursula's resentment. But the farm – it had to be there when they all came back. It was the only thing she could do for her sons. And they must step up to the increased demands from the government to produce more food. She shook her head at the situation. There were no simple answers. That was clear. She went back inside to prepare the lunchtime meal.

Ursula had gone out to the chicken coop to gather eggs, wanting to be alone with her anger. It was a torment that he was always around, and now he would be eating in their kitchen! She wanted him far away from her. She wanted to erase whatever had passed between them in October.

She was trying to stay away from him, to be cold and distant – and here was her mother inviting him to lunch. She couldn't bear to look at him.

And yet, she constantly sought him out, wondering where he was, what he was doing – in order to avoid him, she told herself.

Everything he did infuriated her. He fixed the tractor after she had so struggled with it. He finished chopping the wood for her, as if she were incapable. She told herself it was his Nazi arrogance, wanting to put her in her place.

At least she had succeeded in keeping a distance between them. Two days ago, the prisoners were sitting on the fence as they waited for Zack Wells. She came from the barn, carrying a heavy milk can. Seeing her struggle, Friedrich had jumped down to help her. She'd quickly set the can down, and stood with her palm raised. "I don't need your help," she'd said firmly. She was sure he understood her meaning.

From that day, he kept out of her way. If their paths happened to cross, he averted his eyes. At least he had sense enough for that, she thought. Today when he saw her coming, he had purposely turned away and walked back inside the barn. It was becoming clear to Ursula that he was trying to avoid her. Which was starting to bother her. What right did *he* have to avoid *her*?

The chickens gathered at her feet, where she was scattering feed. She collected a few eggs from the straw and placed them in her basket. The knot that had lodged inside when she saw him again that first day continued to pull and tighten.

She sought out reasons to despise him, but he gave her nothing to work with. She remained alone in her contempt. Her mother was grateful, and Ed was impressed.

"Ursula!" Kate called from the back door.

Surely her mother didn't expect her to be in the same room with the prisoners. She would rather go without lunch than have him near. She would wait until they were finished and back in the fields.

Ursula felt the distance between her and her mother growing, which pained her. She didn't want to add to her mother's already heavy burdens. But her aversion to Friedrich was not something she could talk about.

*

The following day, Ursula watched from the living room window as Ed, Otto, and the prisoners returned from fixing the last of the fences in the farthest field. She was angry that she had wasted so much time awaiting their return – standing at various windows, glancing at the clock, scanning the horizon.

When the group finally returned at end of day, she saw Otto look up at the sky as if gauging the time, and exchange a few words with Ed. Then he motioned for Gustav and Karl to follow Ed to the granary, and he walked with Friedrich to the barn and handed him a milk pail.

Ursula saw an exchange between them and gathered that Friedrich didn't want to do the milking. Otto laughed and gestured inside the barn, and then went to the granary with the others. She glanced out at Ed and her mother; they were working on a list of supplies for repairing the barn and hadn't noticed the exchange.

Against her better sense, Ursula went out into the farmyard, strode to the barn, and stood in the entrance.

She startled Friedrich, who had been talking gently to one of the cows as it lazily swished its tail. He tensed with expectation.

"Is milking too far below you? Is that it?" she asked, satisfied that her tone and expression conveyed the words he didn't understand. She had grown accustomed to insulting him whenever he was near, though she knew the pettiness of such behavior was beneath her.

He turned his back to her and continued to stroke the cow.

She walked up next to him and pointed to the milk pail. "Well, go ahead. You're so quick to impress everyone with your enthusiasm to work, but as soon as no one's looking you dawdle and talk to the cow." She shook her head in disgust. "You're not a Nazi soldier now, but a prisoner. A farmhand."

She lifted the pail, and shoved it in his hand.

He took it, and met her gaze. Then he slowly sat down on the milk stool next to the cow.

Satisfied, Ursula spun around and left. When she reached the door, she looked back. Friedrich remained sitting, but with no apparent intention of milking the cow.

And yet it wasn't reluctance she saw in him, but something more hesitant. He was sitting on the stool all wrong. It flashed on Ursula that he didn't know how to milk a cow, and a smile of triumph spread across her face. Finally, she had the evidence she had been searching for.

She stepped out into the farmyard, pleased with herself. "Ed!" she hollered. "Come here! Come take a look at our prisoner."

Kate glanced up, angered by the tone of command in Ursula's voice, and by the interruption. Ed needed to have the list before he left so that he could get the supplies in town first thing in the morning. And here was Ursula, ready to slow them down with her petty concerns.

Kate and Ed walked over to the barn.

Ursula pointed to Friedrich. "He's not the farmer he claims to be. He's been lying. He can't even milk a cow!" She crossed her arms in justification.

Ed looked over at the POW. Friedrich sat on the milk stool and appeared to be humiliated. Ed scratched his head. "Now, Ursula, maybe he didn't have to milk cows on his farm."

She dropped her arms. "Why are you defending him? Every farmer knows how to milk a cow. He's not – "

Kate's temper flared. She had had enough. She picked up another pail and shoved it into Ursula's hands. "Then show him how to do it and stop wasting our time!"

Kate and Ed walked back towards the porch, leaving Ursula wide-eyed and speechless.

Ursula hoped that Friedrich hadn't understood what happened. She snatched up another stool and dropped it next to his, muttering in indignation.

"I don't believe it! I have to show a despicable Nazi how to milk a cow." She sat down and gave a brusque demonstration, and then gestured for him to do it.

He hesitated a moment, and then made an awkward attempt, but to no avail.

She shook her head impatiently. "Watch. Like this." Again, she showed him.

And again he pulled and squeezed with no result.

"No, like this!" She took his hands, intending to show him once more.

His body reacted with a jolt when her fingers slipped over his.

They both froze and looked down at their linked hands. Ursula felt the heat from his hands course through her, up her arms, her chest, and she closed her eyes.

Then she raised her eyes to him. His gaze pierced her, reaching deep inside, just as it had the first time she saw him. Her breathing became shallow, and she slowly pulled her hands away, aware that they were trembling.

"I hate you," she whispered in a voice that strained to sound angry. "Do you understand? I hate everything about you." Her eyes softly scanned his mouth, his eyes. "Your voice. Your name. Your face."

His gaze held hers, but it was now tinged with pain.

She continued in a tremulous voice. "I hate you – and all Nazis. You're responsible for the death of my brother. Do you understand?"

Her tone said everything. He slowly nodded, though the expression in his eyes didn't change.

She felt herself slipping, as if whatever had been exchanged through the bus window two months ago now sat between them, strong and unavoidable. Then she stood abruptly, knocking over the milk pail, and stormed out of the barn.

She walked up to Ed, who was just heading towards the barn.

"I can't do it, Ed. I just can't do it." She shook her head, and ran up the porch stairs.

Otto had just come out of the granary with Gustav and Karl and saw that Ursula was upset. He motioned for Gustav to switch places with Friedrich, and hurried over.

"Sorry, Ed. I don't know how that happened. I can't allow any mixing. Well," he said, scratching his cheek, "lunch is different, I suppose. But they'd have my head if they knew I let a prisoner alone with a young girl. I wasn't thinking. I should have had Gustav do the milking. He's a farmer through and through."

Gustav finished up with the milking just as the truck arrived to take the prisoners back to camp. Ursula watched them from the kitchen window, gathering that the others were having a laugh at Friedrich for not knowing how to milk a cow.

When the truck was out of sight, she went outside to find Ed. There he was, sitting on the porch step, reading over the list he and Kate had made. She sat down next to him.

She waited for him to say something, but he remained silent.

"I'm sorry, Ed. I was rude to you."

She looked at him, but his eyes were scanning the farmyard, the fields, the line of trees along the creek, all hushed and still at the end of day.

"I love this time of day," he said.

Ursula softened and smiled. She, too, loved the fading of day, just before evening. A light dusting of snow lay on the corn stubble, making long soft rows of gold and white. The light outside the barn grew yellower in the deepening dusk and added a touch of warmth to the cold evening.

"You know," said Ed, "life is simpler when you plow around the stump."

Ursula's eyebrows pinched together. "I know that. And I'm trying to avoid him – them."

"You're tryin' too hard."

Ursula considered his words and wondered if it were true.

After a few minutes, Ed patted her arm. "I know how you feel, but they're good workers. That one, he may not know how to milk a cow, but he's gettin' things done. That's what he's here for."

"I know. It's just that – It seems so wrong. They're Nazis."

"Well, he's German. That's true enough. But everyone should be given a fair chance. That's what you'd want if the tables were turned. If one of your brothers was taken prisoner."

That Ed was not taking her side, as he usually did, made her realize that he was probably right.

"I'm sorry, Ed. I don't know why I'm having such a hard time with this."

"All that matters is that we keep the farm working. That's all that matters to your mother. And your brothers. All the rest – is just stuff."

Ursula looked at him and smiled sadly, comforted by his tender words.

He stood stiffly, took off his hat, and swatted his leg with it. "Just stuff." His tanned, leathery face broke into a smile. Then he put his hat back on, and went inside to say goodnight.

Chapter 7

❧

Mrs. Kinney called to say that the Boy Scouts meeting for the evening had been cancelled. And since Mrs. Kuntzman's daughter was visiting for a few days, Lillian decided to bring Tommy and Gabriel with her to the hospital as helpers.

She went back and forth between the bedroom and living room, wondering how she could change her lesson plan to include the boys. She hunted the bookshelves for a book on action drawing, but couldn't find it anywhere. Perhaps she would bring her oil crayons and improvise a lesson on color, and let the boys help pass supplies around.

"Mom," said Gabriel, "can I bring my explorer kit when we go to Aunt Annette's?"

Lillian looked up in alarm, ready to say "absolutely not!" Then she envisioned Gabriel lost in the snowy woods where a compass might be of use to him. But did he really know how to use one?

"Don't worry, Mom. I promise I won't go exploring by myself. Only if Uncle Bernie comes with me."

Lillian stuffed the oil crayons into a bag. "We'll talk about packing later. Go and get dressed. Are you ready, Tommy?"

Tommy nodded and plopped down on the couch. "I hope Uncle Bernie lets me shoot his gun." He looked up at Lillian, gauging her mood.

"I want a gun for Christmas," he said.

"You are *not* getting a gun," she replied.

"Why not? Uncle Bernie lets Danny shoot his rifle."

"That's different. He's teaching him how to shoot rabbits and quail."

"Can I shoot when we go up there? I'm old enough."

Lillian sighed. "We'll see."

"I want a sled," said Gabriel. "A big one for that hill behind the orchard."

"All I want," said Tommy, "is to practice shooting so when I'm old enough I can be a sharp-shooter and shoot Germans." He raised an imaginary rifle, looked through the sight, and shot at Gabriel.

"Bang! Got him."

Gabriel grabbed his chest, spun around in agony, and dramatically fell to the floor.

Lillian cast a glance at Tommy. "I've told you before, Tommy, I don't like all that talk about killing."

"I'm only killing Germans, Mom."

"And you can't talk about all Germans in one breath," she added.

"Yeah," said Gabriel. "Look at Mrs. Kuntzman. She's German, and she's just like having a real grandmother."

"But we know her. That's different," said Tommy.

Lillian stuffed a few extra materials into her bag for the class. "And don't forget your own heritage, Tommy."

His imaginary gun crumpled into dust. "What do you mean?"

"You have German blood in you. Quite a bit, actually. Along with some Irish and English, and a little French."

"How much?" Tommy asked, concerned.

"Well, your father's maternal grandmother came from Cologne, and his father was mostly German. And there's German on both sides of my family. If you add it all up – at least half, more likely three quarters."

Tommy stood with his mouth open. "You mean – I'm *German?*"

Lillian smiled and ruffled his hair. "Well, no more than you're English or Irish or French."

Tommy stared down at his shoes, wondering what it all meant.

Gabriel raised his arm to Tommy. "Heil Hitler!"

Tommy swatted down his arm. "Knock it off, Gabriel. If I'm part German, then so are you."

"*I'm* American," said Gabriel.

"That's right," laughed Lillian. "Most Americans have their roots in other places, but once you've been here a while you become American." She looked at the boys. "Go comb your hair, Gabriel. You're due for a haircut."

Tommy sat on the couch, cracking his knuckles. "Do you think we still have relatives there?"

"I'm sure we do, somewhere," said Lillian, packing up her supplies.

"But Mom – they could be with the Gestapo. Or SS." He looked back at the floor, and started popping the knuckles on his other hand.

A loud knock at the door caused Tommy to jump.

Lillian exchanged a glance with him. "Who could that be?" She set her bag down and opened the door.

There stood her neighbor, Mrs. Wilson, from down the street, holding a tin of tea.

"Hello, Mrs. Wilson. What a nice surprise!" Lillian immediately noticed the blue cap that sat atop her graying curls, a decided change from her usual head scarf.

"Evening! I was just getting a few things for dinner at the store, and Mrs. Mancetti said this tea just came in for you. I told her I'd bring it over to you."

"Why, thank you, but there was no need to trouble yourself, I could have – "

"I insisted. The truth is I wanted an excuse to stop by. I wanted you to be one of the first to know."

Mrs. Wilson saw Tommy on the couch and leaned around. "Hello, Tommy! Well, what do you think?" She pulled the cap down rakishly over one eye.

Tommy got up and went to the door. "Hi, Mrs. Wilson. Nice cap."

Lillian peered closer and tried to make out the letters on the cap.

Mrs. Wilson cast her eyes up at the brim and adjusted it a little higher on her head. "I've taken a job with the City. I'm going to be a train conductor! Well, a subway train conductor."

Lillian stood open-mouthed. "Why, that's wonderful!" Mrs. Wilson was always busy with volunteer work, but Lillian had never known her to work at a real job – a paying job. It seemed right that she was finally being compensated.

"Harry wasn't too thrilled about it at first, but all the women are working. I have to do my part." She leaned in and whispered. "Course when I told him the salary I'd be making, he changed his tune."

Lillian laughed. "When do you start?"

"I start training on Monday. Well, I just wanted to let you know. Better hurry home and get dinner ready for Harry." She started down the steps, and then turned around. "Who knows – maybe I'll work my way up to a real train conductor. All aboard!" she called, pulling down an imaginary whistle cord. Then she waved goodbye and continued down the stairs.

Lillian said goodnight and closed the door. "Imagine that! Mrs. Wilson working as a subway train conductor." She ruffled Tommy's hair again. "Go tell Gabriel to hurry – we need to leave."

In the bathroom, Gabriel dampened his hair, a sparkle of mischief in his eye. He smiled in the mirror, parted his hair on the far left, and combed it smooth over his forehead. Then he placed the short black comb under his nose to look like a moustache, and tried his best to look severe.

Tommy went to the bathroom to get Gabriel. "Come on, Gabe, we're –" He stopped mid-sentence. There was Gabriel – a small version of Hitler.

Gabriel clicked his heels together. "Cousin Adolph here."

Tommy pulled the comb down. "I said knock it off, Gabriel. It's not funny."

Gabriel grabbed his comb back and began imitating Tommy, biting his nails in terror. "Vhat you mean – *I'm German?*"

Tommy snatched the comb and pushed Gabriel, who shoved him back and grabbed at the comb. They were soon rolling in the hallway, throwing punches. Tommy quickly gained the upper hand and pinned Gabriel down.

"Ow!" laughed Gabriel. "Get off me."

Lillian was pulling on her coat when she heard the commotion. "Tommy, Gabriel! Stop that right now!"

Gabriel tried to twist out of the hold, and winced at the punch that landed on his arm. "Ow, that hurt! See what a mean Nazi bully you are?"

Tommy's fist froze in mid-air. He slowly rolled off Gabriel.

Lillian put her hands on her hips. "That's enough! Come on, we're going to be late."

Gabriel sat up, shaking his head. "We're American, you dope. Why are you making such a big deal about it?"

"Come on, boys. Put your coats on. How many times do I have to tell you, Tommy, fighting is not the answer to everything. It's turning into a habit with you."

Tommy angrily pulled on his coat, and they left the apartment in a hurry.

Gabriel quickly forgot the tussle as he ran down the stairs ahead of them. He waited at the entry. "I wish Dad was coming with us for Christmas. Do you think he'll be home in time, Mom? I bet he's going to surprise us with a visit while we're up at the orchard. Then he can help us find a tree and chop it down and bring it – "

"No, Gabriel." Lillian had wanted to wait before she told the boys, but decided that now was perhaps the best time, with the distraction of going to the hospital. "I finally had a letter today – actually three letters arrived all at once. I'll read them to you when we get back home." She had to wait a moment to make sure her voice was steady. "He said he won't be home any time soon. Not for the next few months anyway."

"You mean he's going to miss Christmas?" asked Gabriel.

Tommy tried to read her face. "Are you sure, Mom?"

She put her arms around their shoulders as they walked to the bus stop. "Yes, I'm sure. He wrote that he hopes we go to Annette and Bernie's for Christmas and to have some hot spiced cider for him. And to write to him about all the things we do there."

Tommy saw the sadness in her face, and in Gabriel's. "Like sledding, Gabe. I'll take you down the big hill this time. Last time we were there you were too little, remember?"

Gabriel smiled up at Tommy. "And we'll go ice skating."

"And roast chestnuts, and drink hot chocolate," said Tommy.

"With whipped cream!" Gabriel said, holding up his finger as if not to forget the important part. "Aunt Annette always makes whipped cream."

They climbed onto the bus, and while the boys talked about building snow forts and making a bonfire by the pond and playing with Danny and their cousins, Lillian stared out the window.

Charles's letter had brought her happiness that he was alive and well, but the certainty that he wouldn't be home for months struck her like a blow. Who knew how long it would be before she was in his arms again? The war was raging on, the Allies were gaining the upper hand, but would it last? Did the Germans have a secret weapon as rumored? Would the recent victories turn into defeats? Would Charles come home at all?

She put her hand over her mouth, and then sat up straight. He would come home. And she would be there waiting for him.

*

The number of Lillian's students had increased with each class, and she had agreed to give lessons two nights a week and on Saturday afternoons – at least for the month of December when the need for keeping spirits up was greater. Lillian was pleased to find that a few of the newer students had experience with drawing and were able to help out the other students.

Tommy and Gabriel had fast become favorites of the class. This was the third time Lillian had brought them, and she found that having them there added to the merriment of the group. Tommy clearly enjoyed the company of the men and liked to hear their humorous stories, and Gabriel felt important in his role as helper. Lillian found that, for the most part, the men were respectful and watched their language when the boys were around.

Tonight Lillian insisted that, rather than depict her, as she had allowed in the earlier sessions, the soldiers sketch each other, so that she could freely move about the room. Some of the men began to grumble about drawing each other.

Sergeant Remling threw his pencil down after trying to draw Memphis, a cheerful lanky fellow with buck teeth. "How am I ever supposed to learn how to draw a woman if I don't practice on one?"

Lillian looked up at the unexpected outburst. "Well, the principles are the same and – "

"Yeah," shouted the young man called Rossi. "How we supposed to draw our mothers and sisters if we only have these ugly mugs to practice on?"

Bushwick, the man he was sketching, joined in. "Yeah, his sister's none too beautiful to behold as it is, and if he makes her any uglier . . ." He shook his head in horror.

"She's not as ugly as *your* sister," Rossi countered.

The two men escalated their insults, to the amusement of the others.

Remling leaned against the desk and pointed to the men. "Can't you see? We're tired of drawing each other. Don't you have a friend you could bring in?"

Lillian understood what he was getting at and smiled. "That's a wonderful idea. I'm sure the boys' babysitter would be happy to come in and model for you."

Remling leaned over to Tommy and whispered. "How old is she?"

Tommy thought about it. "I'm not sure, but she has white hair."

Remling and the others groaned in exaggerated despair, holding their heads.

"Hey, Mom," said Gabriel. "How about Izzy?" He turned to some of the patients. "She's real pretty and has red hair."

"And a nice figure?" asked Vinnie.

Gabriel shrugged. "I guess so."

Vinnie caught Lillian's warning look and held up his hands in apology.

"We promise to mind our manners," said Remling, smacking Vinnie on the shoulder.

"Best behavior and all that," added Rossi, his hands clasped in prayer.

"I'm inspired just by the thought," said Bushwick.

Lillian looked out at the room of hopeful faces. "Well," she said, "I suppose you have a point. I certainly don't want to be held responsible for unflattering family portraits. Perhaps I can persuade her to come in one night."

She laughed at the cheers. "I can't make any promises."

When the class finished, she instructed Tommy and Gabriel to help Mrs. Coppel set up for the next class, while she went upstairs to the bedridden patients.

"Tommy, Gabriel – half an hour," she called from the door.

But they barely took note of her departure. They sat in the middle of the men, immersed in a story involving a camp commander, and were laughing at Vinnie's imitation of him.

Lillian didn't allow Tommy and Gabriel to attend the private lesson upstairs. She was afraid it would be too upsetting for them. Some of the men were pretty badly injured – disfigured, and dejected.

She had worked with a few different patients in the ward, but lately two men in particular showed some real interest – Mr. Carmichael, an older man, who had taken art classes years ago, and Ernest

Weiss, a very young man with longing in his eyes, who always talked to Lillian about his family.

After spending some time with Mr. Carmichael, she went to Ernest's bedside. His face lit up and he showed her his recent sketches – some were of other patients, while others depicted memories from home. After spending about fifteen minutes with him, encouraging him on his progress and making a few suggestions, she got up to leave.

He reached out and took her hand. "Please. Stay a little longer."

Lillian tried to read his expression. Loneliness. Poor boy, she thought. He was from a large family and was utterly homesick.

"I was hoping we could start working with color," he said.

Lillian smiled and patted his hand. "All right," she said, reaching for her oil crayons. "Let's start with these."

He lifted his eyes, and carefully watched her as she explained how to layer and shade.

Chapter 8

∾

Ursula felt blown by raw, wild impulses. And she couldn't still the storm long enough to look at it carefully – to analyze it and take some disciplined action against it. The fears and worries that daily and nightly twisted inside her were beginning to wear her down. It was becoming work to try to avoid him. He would appear in her dreams, and she would awake with a start – and then try to quickly fall back asleep in hope that the dream would continue. And no matter the outcome, she awoke in the morning, torn between disappointment and guilt.

She had kept up the denial of her feelings, until the day she had tried to teach him how to milk the cow – and then, unexpectedly, the tightly closed box of the October day had sprung open, unfurling her heart all over again. Over and over she replayed that day in the barn, and, as much as she wanted to, she couldn't blame him for anything. It was she who had gone into the barn. She who had placed her hands over his.

Ursula hated herself for thinking about him, for seeking him out. She told herself it was because she detested him and was watching for signs of Nazi treachery. But the pretense was beginning to wear thin.

She stayed away from him, watching him from the upstairs window. Sometimes she would see him stand and gaze out over the fields, and she sensed a look of sadness in his face, in the way he stood. On two occasions, she saw him pull a photo from his pocket, and she felt a stab of heat shoot through her. A photo of his wife? His fiancée?

Driven by a host of unanswered questions, she took to asking Ed about him, careful to include questions about the other prisoners, as well. Were they all married? What else did he know about them? She always concluded her questioning by expressing her displeasure: "I know they're helping. I can see that. I just wish they weren't German."

Ursula grew more desperate, and try as she might to find something she could fault Friedrich with, he gave her nothing to fuel her fire. He was kind and generous, sensitive and hard-working. And though she hated to admit it, he was beautiful – in a way that spoke to her, as it had that day in October.

A beauty that spoke of hidden depths. She wished he were unappealing and dull. But there was intelligence in his eyes, suppressed emotion. He was strong and angular, yet there was tenderness in his ways. She had seen it again and again – almost a protectiveness of the others. Always taking the heavier jobs, always showing a respectful manner towards Ed and Otto, towards her mother. And like the others, he was good-natured. He smiled to everyone – but her. And also like the others, he sang while he worked – beautifully. She had heard him on several occasions, his voice rich and –

A surge of anger welled up in her – what was she thinking? He was the enemy. He was a Nazi. She had to keep that thought foremost in her mind. It was a betrayal to see the kindness in him, to admire him in any way. Though it went against her nature, she would learn how to hate, or at least how to sharpen her faculties for disdain.

It didn't help that everyone seemed to be softening towards the POWs. Her mother and sister were growing friendlier with them, Ed and Otto seemed to enjoy their company – what was wrong with everyone?

And yet, here on the farm, working with them almost every day, it was hard not to see them as individuals, and understand that they all missed their homes, their loved ones. Again, she remembered how Friedrich had looked at the photograph.

She imagined a beautiful German girl, waiting for him. Waiting to be back in his arms – waiting to feel the heat and strength of his embrace, his lips touching –

She strode out of her room, furious that she couldn't keep her mind fixed. He was turning into something other than the enemy. They all were. They were becoming familiar, God curse them all. How could she and the others forget that these men belonged to the army that killed Francis?

And now they were sharing their kitchen with them? Ursula had pleaded with her mother, and at first Kate had agreed to feed them out on the enclosed back porch. But over the past few days, the temperature had dropped and Kate insisted to Otto that they all eat inside. Otto was grateful, but said that the men were hesitant.

So far Ursula had avoided the kitchen when the POWs were there. But today, she wanted to see them to let them know that they were prisoners and not favored guests.

She went downstairs, angry at the cheerful voices and laughter flowing from the kitchen. It was Saturday, and Shirley was over again. She had been spending more and more time at the house, telling Jessica how nice it was that her POWs were young and handsome. And she took pleasure in practicing the few German words she had learned. But today, her playful voice grated on Ursula.

They were all losing sight of the real nature of the situation.

From the living room, she saw that Jessica and Shirley were serving the food, and they had the audacity to giggle at Karl who was trying to make sense of a ridiculous song playing on the radio.

He listened intently to the song, turning his face to one side, then the other, as if to better catch the words – but he remained puzzled. "Is English?"

Otto tried to explain that it was a nonsense song. "Mairzy Doats." He tried to break it down for Karl, in long, loud syllables. "Mares. Mares, eat, oats." When Karl still showed no comprehension, Otto mimed a horse being fed.

Karl's face lit up in sudden understanding. "Ah! Is about a horse!"

Which sent Jessica and Shirley into peals of laughter. Even Kate and Ed joined in. Ursula saw Friedrich's face softening at the merriment.

It was too much for her. She stomped into the kitchen.

"Jessica!" she snapped.

Jessica raised her head at the rebuke, and left the room with Shirley, their suppressed giggles trailing behind them.

Kate threw Ursula a sharp look. But Ed wore a curious expression, as if seeing something else – and when their eyes met, Ursula felt the blood rush to her cheeks. Soon Friedrich and the two other prisoners stood, thanked Kate, and left the kitchen to go back outside.

Ed pushed himself up from the table, and took his hat from the coat-rack. "I'll be out in the barn."

Kate began clearing the table, banging the dishes. Ursula stood with her arms crossed, wondering if she had gone too far – and wondering why she was becoming more and more impulsive.

Kate turned to her. "There's enough tension in our lives without you adding to it. Why do you begrudge the girls a little happiness? Why hurt these three men who are so far from home? Put yourself in their place."

Ursula went back upstairs and shut her bedroom door. Then, parting the curtain, she watched the men from her window. Gustav and Karl were laughing as they loaded up the wagon. Friedrich took out the photo, looked at it, and then slipped it back into his shirt pocket, before following the others into the barn. A flash of anger shot through Ursula – she wanted to rip the photo in two.

Instead, she went to the mirror and studied her reflection.

"I'm just a farm girl," she said. She compared herself to the imagined beautiful and cultured German girl in the photo.

With one hand, she twisted her hair up and raised her chin to better see her amethysts – but her earrings seemed a mockery. She dropped her hand in disappointment. There was a time, not so long ago, when she had been proud of her appearance. When she had brushed her chestnut-colored hair until it gleamed like buckeyes. When she had dressed up for the dances, her trim figure set off by a pretty dress, and was secretly gratified by the admiring glances.

But she no longer cared about all that. She even wondered if those days were gone. If she had already lost her looks. Dungarees and overalls, her brothers' shirts, heavy work shoes – that was her look nowadays.

In rebellion against that image, she stripped off her work clothes, opened the closet, and pulled out the blue satin dress that best brought out the deep blue of her eyes and showed her figure. She stepped into the dress, and brushed her hair. Even went so far as to put on stockings and her good shoes.

Then she looked into the mirror, and tried a smile. Thank God. A hint of prettiness was still there – if she smiled. That's what was missing – the softness that a smile brought. She had a hard look these days. She smiled again, and brought it back. Then frowned. She hated vanity in other girls – and yet, as she studied her silhouette, her face, she was glad that whatever beauty she had was still there. It wasn't vanity, was it? To want to feel pretty, in the way a summer day could be pretty, or the night sky? To want to be a part of life, instead of feeling like she was stuck out on the edges, watching the world pass by. Soon she would be eighteen. Then nineteen. Then –

She heard a truck outside, went to the window, and groaned. There was Joe Madden, calling on her again. She thought he had gotten the message and would leave her alone, and move on to Sue Ellen.

Ed walked out of the barn and went over to greet him, while Otto and the prisoners looked on.

The contrariness that her mother always accused her of now stubbornly rose up inside Ursula. She ran downstairs, past her astonished mother, sister, and Shirley, and opened the door to the brisk December day.

Joe was just coming up to the house. Ursula stood on the porch and waited for him, aware of the breeze fluttering her dress, aware of the eyes on her.

"Well, look at that!" remarked Shirley, with her hands on her hips.

Jessica shook her head. "She goes from one extreme to the other!"

Kate exchanged a glance with Jessica, and then went onto the porch where Ursula and Joe stood talking.

"Afternoon, Joe!" called Kate. "Come inside where it's warm." She gave Ursula a look of reprimand as Joe stepped inside.

"Jessica, fix Joe a slice of that pie and a cup of hot coffee – since your sister seems to have lost her good mind."

Jessica stared at Ursula, dressed up in the middle of the work day. "What are you all dolled up for?"

Ursula frowned at Jessica's choice of words. "Hardly all dolled up. Just seeing if I had anything to wear to the dance."

"So you're going?" asked Joe, his face brightening. "That's what I came to ask you about."

"I – I haven't decided yet," said Ursula, already regretting her folly.

"Sue Ellen said she wouldn't miss it for the world," said Shirley. "Everyone is going to be there."

The hope in Joe's earnest face filled Ursula with shame.

"I'll be right back." She ran upstairs, baffling everyone, and changed back into her dungarees and flannel work shirt. She parted the lace curtains at her window and glanced down at the barn; Friedrich had his eyes fixed on the farmhouse door.

Ursula clomped downstairs in her heavy shoes, transformed back into homespun farmhand, and joined the others at the table.

"How've you been faring, Joe?" she asked. "How's your mother?"

A conversation followed about the Christmas preparations for the USO in town and the upcoming Christmas dance at the town hall. Ursula listened politely, but she let Jessica and Shirley do most of the talking.

Kate gave Jessica a discreet nod, and got up from the table. "Jessica, Shirley, come help me bring the rest of that pie out to the others. And some coffee."

Ursula understood the intention of leaving her and Joe alone and resented it. She wished she had never indulged in such impulsive behavior. There was good-hearted Joe getting his hopes up for nothing. It was wrong of her. It was beneath her – and so unfair to Joe.

In the middle of his talking about some of their classmates who would be at the dance, Ursula suddenly interrupted him.

"I'm sorry, Joe. I – I don't think I'll be going to the dance, after all."

Crestfallen, he turned a perplexed gaze to Ursula, as if he couldn't keep up with all her twists and turns.

He was too honest and good-natured to play with. "I don't feel much like dancing these days," Ursula explained. "Why don't you ask Sue Ellen? Everyone knows she's fond of you."

Joe nodded, understanding everything in those words. He took a sip of coffee and set his cup down.

"Perhaps I will. I guess there comes a point where a fella has to accept things and move on." He tapped his stiff leg. "That's one thing I learned from this. But will you save me a dance if you decide to go?"

"I can't promise that – you'll be in high demand, Joe. There won't be many handsome young men for the girls to dance with – and a hero at that."

Joe grinned at the compliment. And they soon slipped into a relaxed conversation, more in the vein of the old friendship they had always enjoyed.

They then walked back to the porch, and said their goodbyes. As Ursula watched him walk with the war limp he would always have, she hoped that he would find what that they were all in search of. Love. Tenderness. Someone who answered the deep yearning inside and who made the world a lovely place.

Shirley ran up to him, seeing an opportunity to further her sister's cause. "Leaving Joe? Can you give me a lift home? I know Sue Ellen would be happy to see you."

"Sure. Hop on in." He said goodbye to the others, nodded at Ursula, and drove off.

Ursula stood on the porch and waved good-bye to him. When she looked over towards the barn, she saw Friedrich turn away and enter the barn. Ashamed of herself on account of both men, Ursula spun around, and went back inside.

Out in the barn, Otto poured himself another cup of coffee. "And who was that handsome young buck calling at the house?"

"That was Joe Madden," answered Kate. "You remember him, don't you?"

"Haven't seen him in years. Isn't he the one who – "

Ed nodded. "Wounded at Guadalcanal, after bringing several men to safety. Been sweet on Ursula for years. Come to ask her to the dance."

"He's just wasting his time," said Jessica.

"You don't know that," said Kate, though she was afraid it was true. Yet she hoped that the dress and brightness in Ursula's face were signs of a return to happiness – a kind of happiness anyway.

"You know it's true, Mom. She won't go with him."

Kate shook her head. "Well, I don't know what she's waiting for. Joe's a good, honest farmer. She could do no better."

"It's always been that way," said Jessica. "Sue Ellen says Ursula could have any boy she wants, but she never cares about them. She said it's because Ursula thinks she's better than them."

Ed saw a flash of anger surface in Kate. "Well, Ursula's particular, is all," he said. "No rush."

"But it's always like that," said Jessica. "The boys fall in love with her, and she just ignores them. It's not fair."

"And just what is she supposed to do?" asked Kate. "Court them all? Encourage them all? That's not her way. Unlike Sue Ellen – always angling for attention."

"Now, Kate," said Ed, keeping things in balance. "Sue Ellen's all right. She'll make a good farmer's wife."

"She's had a crush on Joe for years," added Jessica. "She bought a cookbook and has been practicing. She read that the way to a man's heart is through his stomach. Shirley says she's always trying out some new recipe."

"I guess that'll work on some men," said Ed.

"All I'm saying," continued Jessica, "is that most girls would be plenty happy if Joe Madden asked them to the dance. Sue Ellen has tried everything to make him notice her. She picked out that purple calico way back in October and has been slaving over that dress. And she's going to have her hair set at the beauty parlor so that she'll have some curls for the dance."

"That's my point," said Kate.

"Someone has to get things going," said Jessica. "How else are people supposed to pair up?"

"Well, I'm glad Ursula's not like that," Kate said.

"She doesn't have to be," Jessica responded. "The boys flock to her like bees to honey."

Kate threw her a look, and Jessica decided that enough had been said. Kate collected the plates and returned to the house, while Ed and the others continued with their work.

Friedrich stood at the barn entrance, looking at the house.

Jessica observed him, amused – knowing that he had understood the gist of their conversation. She saw his chest rise and fall faster, as if agitated. She shook her head and gathered the thermos and cups. "Like bees to honey," she said.

*

Just as the sun was lowering over the fields, Ursula took a large basket and went outside to gather up the laundry that was snapping in the cold December breeze. She unpinned the sheets, and tossed them into the basket. She heard laughter coming from the front of the house where the prisoners and Ed and Otto were waiting for Zack Wells.

She walked to the barn so that she could watch them, unobserved. But when she stepped through the side door, she stopped – there was

Friedrich, only a few feet from her, looking at the hateful photograph.

When he saw her, he quickly put the photo back in his shirt pocket and stiffened, as if in defense at the unpredictable behavior of this girl.

Ursula walked up to him. "Who are you always looking at? It that your Nazi *fräulein?*"

His jaw clenched, but Ursula came closer towards him. Believing that his anger was in defense of his beautiful woman back home made Ursula even more reckless. Everything he did made her angry and impetuous. He was the cause of all her pain and confusion and the tangle of misery inside her. She wanted nothing more than to provoke him.

"Despicable Nazis," she said, gesturing to the photo.

His fists tightened at his sides and his chest rose and fell. Gratified, Ursula moved even closer to him.

"What? Are you going to hurt me? Is that why you're here?" Though he might not understand her words, she was sure he understood her contempt. She lightly pushed at his chest.

He took a step back, surprised by her action.

Though she would later wonder at her boldness, she stepped up to him, their bodies almost touching, and raised her chin.

"I'm not afraid of you. You Nazis are nothing but cowards. It was someone like you who killed my brother!" She intended to turn and never speak to him again.

But he suddenly grabbed her arm and drew her so close that she could feel the heat from his body. Then in near-perfect English he spoke.

"You think you're the only one who has lost someone? You think you're the only one to feel pain? You carry around your loss like a trophy that separates you from everyone else."

Ursula's eyes widened, shocked that he was speaking English. Shocked at his words. Shocked at the voltage running from his hand through her body. She pulled her arm away from his grip, but he then clutched her chin.

"And don't you *ever* call me a Nazi – you stupid girl!"

Then his face broke and his eyes filled with pain or sadness – she didn't know which. He was about to say something more, but instead, he quickly turned and left.

Ursula stood trembling, her arms around herself, not sure of what just happened. Then she unsteadily backed up and sat on a bale of hay, her cheeks still burning. Stunned, she looked to where he had exited the barn.

She heard Zack's truck arrive and ran to the entrance of the barn.

Friedrich and the others climbed into the back, and soon the truck pulled away.

She waited in vain for him to turn around. The truck was almost out of vision – but still he did not look back.

*

Still reeling from the encounter, Ursula was unable to eat dinner, saying she didn't feel well. She took a bath and went to her room early.

But Jessica didn't want to let things rest. She walked into to Ursula's room and sat down on her bed.

"Joe's a nice boy, Ursula. I hope you didn't hurt his feelings."

"Joe and I are friends. We always have been," Ursula said, somewhat defensively. "But I hope I didn't hurt him," she added. "He's been through so much."

Ursula began brushing her hair, avoiding Jessica's watchful eyes. "Joe understands. He knows that he's more like a brother to me. That's how I see him. I can't help it. You'll be happy to know that I encouraged him to ask Sue Ellen to the dance."

"Hmm. I wonder why."

Ursula glanced at her sister. "I thought you would be happy."

"I am."

Jessica waited, carefully watching Ursula brushing her hair, her mind clearly elsewhere.

"Why do you always watch him?" Jessica asked.

Ursula looked up, startled by the simple question. "Who are you talking about?"

"You know who I'm talking about."

Ursula flushed crimson and turned to face her sister. "No, I don't. Who do you mean?"

Jessica tilted her head to the side. "I'm not a baby, you know. I see you watching him all the time. Friedrich."

Ursula turned back around. "I don't. No more than I watch the others. I don't trust them. And you should be more cautious."

"They're nice – all of them."

"You should keep your distance." Ursula brushed her hair vigorously. "I don't like to see you and Shirley so open and friendly with them."

"Don't worry. We know you want him for yourself."

Ursula spun around. "How dare you say such a thing!"

Jessica immediately regretted her words, but was not backing down now.

"Don't be stupid, Ursula. I see how he watches you. His eyes follow you everywhere. You should have seen his face when Joe stopped by. I thought he was going to explode – or cry. It's like he's in l –"

"Stop it!"

"As usual, you've cast your spell."

"Don't talk such foolishness! He's the enemy. Do you understand? Don't you *ever* say anything like that again!"

"All right, I won't. But that won't stop it from being true." Jessica got up and went to her room, happy that she had her answer.

Ursula was pulled violently in two directions. Shameful joy at Jessica's words – and anguish that perhaps she was revealing something that she didn't dare name even to herself.

She looked at her arms, seeing once again his hands on her. She remembered her hand on his chest – and how she had wanted to keep it there.

She put her face in her hands, hating herself for wanting to melt into him. She was no better than a traitor – to her brother, to herself, to her country.

The only thing to do was to stay away from him. She had behaved recklessly. Ever since she was a little girl, everyone told her that she was mature for her age. Now here she was, behaving like a foolish schoolgirl. No wonder he despises me, she thought. No wonder he thinks of me as stupid.

She would never behave like that again. Nor would she give cause for anyone to think she was capable of such treachery. She would learn to control herself, to hide her feelings. It must be possible.

Chapter 9

As Lillian overheard Izzy and Mr. Rockwell arguing, she reminded herself how lucky she was to work upstairs in the Art Department. The days when she had worked at the switchboard on the main floor of Rockwell Publishing had always been fraught with the ups and downs of Mr. Rockwell. For the past few years, Izzy had borne the brunt of his difficult ways, but she was fast losing her tolerance.

Rockwell waved his cigar as he tried to bully Izzy into staying late to finish up on a project.

"You can't or you won't?" he demanded.

Izzy ignored him as she busily delivered a few papers back and forth between his secretary and a few other harried employees.

Rockwell was right on her heels. "I asked you a question! Are you unable or unwilling?"

Izzy stopped and gave him her full attention. She tapped her cheek and gazed up at the ceiling, carefully pondering his question. "Unwilling." She took her purse from her desk drawer, and grabbed her coat and hat.

"Fine, then!" Rockwell stormed. "Enjoy your evening, Miss Briggs!"

"I intend to, Mr. Rockwell!" Izzy called after him, and left the room. She greeted Lillian with an angry shake of her head as she pulled on her coat.

"I tell you Lilly that man is going to meet my fist before the year is out. Does it matter that I have stayed late almost every night since the war broke out? Does it matter that I have attended every one of his tiresome galas? No. All that matters to him is that today I said, 'No, I can't stay late.'"

Izzy wound up her fist, ready to let him have it. "I told him, 'Go ahead and fire me – I'll get a factory job and make double what you're paying me.' That shut him up. For a while."

"You wouldn't really do that, would you, Izzy?"

"I would, and he knows it. Look at how many of the girls have left here. Maureen, she's a welder, and making good money. Gloria is over at the shipyards and has already been promoted. Why I stay slaving for that man is beyond me."

"My neighbor down the street, Mrs. Wilson, has taken a job as a subway train conductor – can you imagine?"

Izzy considered the image, and smiled. "Actually I can. She's a very capable woman. I can see her running the whole Transportation Department."

Lillian nodded. "I know what you mean. She was born to lead, organize, and command." She rubbed Izzy's arm. "Don't let Mr. Rockwell get to you. He's just come to depend on you so much."

"Rockwell who? All I'm thinking about right now is Archie, and that in," she glanced at her watch, "thirty minutes, I'm going to be sitting at a restaurant with a checked tablecloth and a lit candle. Then out to a dance. And every night until he leaves. I told him he can visit his family in the day, but from six o'clock until midnight, he's all mine." Izzy told Lillian about the clubs and restaurants they had already gone to, and her plans for the next several nights.

Lillian tilted her head to look at Izzy, once again surprised that she wanted to go to all the old places that she and Red used to frequent. She would have thought –

"What?" asked Izzy.

Lillian shook her head and looked away.

"Tell me – I know you're thinking something about what I just said."

"Nothing, really. It's just that – those are all the places you and Red used to go. I didn't think you'd want – "

"That's because they're the best places in the city. Come on, let's get out of here."

They crossed the busy lobby and stepped out into the cold December evening. Izzy, brightening at the prospect of seeing Archie, linked her arm with Lillian's and squeezed it in joy.

"I'm falling hard, Lilly. I've spent almost every night out with him since he's been back, and it's still going great. Don't you think that means something?"

"Like what?" Lillian asked, trying to interpret the sparkle in Izzy's eye.

"I'm not sure, but – I have a feeling he might ask me something tonight. Or soon."

Lillian stopped and faced her. "You mean – propose? So soon?"

"It's not so soon. We've been writing to each other for months. Some women are getting married to soldiers after just a few days of meeting them. Life is uncertain, furloughs are short and getting scarce. You have to grab what comes your way."

Lillian didn't want to burst her bubble, but something didn't feel right. It felt too much like a replay. Izzy hadn't been this happy since – since her engagement to Red. "Well, I can't wait to meet him."

"I told him you would be there on Saturday – you can't back out."

"I'll be there, I promise. The boys have their sleepover after Scouts with Mickey and Billy and a few other boys. Mr. Kinney is helping them earn their badge – they'll be putting on a hospital Christmas show for the soldiers, and then camp out in the bomb shelter and eat GI ration food. So I have the whole night open."

"It'll be good for you to get out."

"I get out all the time now. I teach three times a week. I'm getting to know my students better, and I find that I really enjoy teaching. Though sometimes I think they're more interested in talking than in drawing. But I've made sketches for a few of them that they sent home, and there's a handful of them that sincerely want to learn."

"They must love having a gorgeous woman as their instructor."

"Oh, Izzy. I'm sure they don't see me like that."

Izzy looked at Lillian from under her brow. "Trust me, that's *exactly* how they see you."

"Well, there are a few cads, just good-natured teasing. But you can tell they're just lonely."

"Lonely for female company." Izzy cut in over Lillian's objection. "Lilly, they've been away for months, years even. You can't blame them."

"Well, most of them are perfect gentlemen." Lillian thought of Ernest and smiled. "There's one boy, with a leg wound, who looked so sad when

I first met him. But he's really cheered up lately and so looks forward to the lessons. And he's a fast learner. The doctor told one of the nurses that the art instructions are helping his disposition. He's been much more cheerful since the drawing classes."

"I don't think it's the art, Lilly."

"Of course it is. It's very therapeutic."

Izzy opened her mouth to say something, but changed her mind.

"That reminds me, Izzy. I have a huge favor to ask. I don't want to cut into your time with Archie, but do you think you could stop by the hospital one night while I teach? My students are requesting a female model to draw, and I thought you would be perfect."

"Aha! So you do understand our boys!" she laughed. "I take it you didn't ask Mrs. Wilson or Mrs. Kuntzman."

"Well, no – I…" Lillian looked down, aware that Izzy was right.

Izzy gave another laugh. "I'd love nothing more. How about this Saturday? I can stop by your class before meeting up with Archie. And you can join us when you're finished."

"That'd be swell, Izzy. I know it will mean a lot to them."

They parted at the corner. "I can't wait for you to meet Archie – you're going to love him!" Izzy ran to catch the downtown bus.

*

Lillian stopped by Mancetti's on her way home, and was shifting the bag of groceries from one arm to another when she saw Mrs. Wilson walking briskly towards her. She raised her head and smiled in greeting.

"Evening, Mrs. Drooms! Getting colder, isn't it? I just passed the boys going home," she said, looking back at Lillian's brownstone. "I told Tommy to put some ice on that eye."

"Oh, not again!" said Lillian, infuriated. "I don't know what's going on with him, fighting all the time. All he talks about is fighter planes and guns. He just got over one black eye – and now another?"

Mrs. Wilson waved away any idea of concern. "It's just a phase. Mark my words, in another year or two he'll have his mind on *other* things, and you'll be wishing for these less complicated boyhood years." She sighed deeply, remembering her own children. "They grow up so fast. Enjoy these years while you can."

Lillian noticed a Christmas brooch on Mrs. Wilson's coat lapel, and that she was wearing dress shoes. "Are you going out tonight?"

"I'm meeting Harry for dinner – can you *believe* it? He's gotten all romantic what with me having a job and all." She leaned closer and placed her hand on Lillian's arm. "I think it's his way of saying that he's going to miss me always being at home for him. If I had known he was going to behave *this* way, I would have gotten a job years ago!" She fluffed up her graying hair coquettishly, and then whipped out her head scarf and tied it under her chin. "Have a good evening, Mrs. Drooms. And for heaven's sake, don't worry about Tommy. Ta-ta!"

When Lillian opened the door to her apartment, she saw that Tommy and Gabriel were in the bathroom. Tommy had a washcloth under his nose, and Gabriel was washing something out in the sink.

"You're in big trouble, Tommy," Gabriel said.

"Just hurry up, Gabe. We have to clean it before Mom sees it."

Lillian walked to the bathroom and stood in the doorway. "Before I see what?" Her anger vanished when she saw the blood on Tommy's T-shirt, and his swollen nose. "Tommy!" She placed one hand on his neck and gently took the washcloth away from his nose to take a look. "What happened this time?"

Tommy took the washcloth back and put it under his nose, wincing. "It's nothing, Mom. I'm okay."

Gabriel avoided her questioning stare and bent over Tommy's soapy shirt in the sink, rubbing it more vigorously.

"Tell me what happened." Lillian had her hands on her hips; the boys knew better than to try to lie.

"Tommy?" she waited for an answer. She turned to Gabriel.

"Salt!" cried Gabriel, escaping to the kitchen. "Salt takes blood out."

Tommy went to the living room and sat on the couch.

Lillian patiently took off her coat and hat and hung them on the hall tree. Then she stood in front of Tommy.

He scrunched up his face, thinking of how to explain. "Well, I kind of had an argument."

"Not at school, I hope!"

"No, after school. On the way home."

Lillian waited, growing impatient that Tommy wasn't volunteering any information.

Then Gabriel came into the living room, the salt shaker in his hand. "It wasn't his fault, Mom. That dope Butch said Hitler could still win the war, and Tommy said 'no he couldn't,' and Butch said 'yes he could,' and Tommy said 'if you're gonna talk stupid you can just shut your mouth' and that's when Butch said 'oh yeah? Make me' so – " Gabriel shrugged his shoulders, the rest of the story being obvious.

"Was he hurt?" Lillian asked, concerned.

"You bet! Tommy clipped him a good one," Gabriel said, with a proud smile.

"Gabriel!" Lillian cried.

"Only after he hit Tommy in the nose and made him bleed," he quickly added.

Lillian sat down next to Tommy, shaking her head. "What am I going to do with you boys? Gabriel running off from school, and you fighting whenever you get a chance."

Tommy had his elbows on his knees, his head in his hands. "Sorry, Mom."

"You convinced me that you were old enough not to need a babysitter after school, but I think – "

"It would have happened anyway," said Tommy. "It started at school."

It was moments like these when she wished Charles were there to help. He would know what to do and be able to explain things to the boys. They always listened to him. The thought of Charles suddenly filled her with sadness. She rose to her feet and glanced at the clock.

"We'll talk about it later. Go change your shirt, and let me fix dinner." Lillian felt she was taking the easy way out, but she just didn't feel like scolding Tommy. Maybe up at Annette's, away from everything, she could talk to him about it.

The boys were soon helping to set the table and seeing what was for dinner. Lillian gave Tommy a quick squeeze as he lifted the lid on the simmering vegetable soup.

He smiled up at her, wondering how he had gotten off so lightly. He and Gabriel exchanged a smile, and lifted their shoulders in bafflement.

*

That night Lillian lay in bed, missing Charles more than ever. She had stayed up late writing him a letter, pouring out her heart to him about Tommy's fighting and Gabriel's skipping school, and writing about her loneliness.

Then she tore it up, and wrote a calmer letter about how well they were all doing, and how the boys were looking forward to having Christmas with their cousins.

It seemed that every day something happened that made her wish Charles were there. She wanted to talk to him about Tommy and Gabriel. She wanted to tell him about the patients and about how surprised she was that she enjoyed teaching so much. She wanted to tell him her idea of perhaps becoming a teacher and trying to find freelance work as an illustrator.

Even though every day seemed to emphasize his being gone, it was the nights that were so difficult. She never knew that a bed could feel so empty, that a night could be so long.

She placed her hand on his pillow, and then pulled it over and laid her cheek on it. She could almost hear the tenderness in his voice, see the smile that always melted her, and that soft look in his eye that was for her alone.

Visions of their early days filled her mind: the excitement she felt on learning something new about him, the thrill of filling in the gaps, of everything that made him more and more hers. She remembered the desperate passion that filled their nights – a wild mix of delight in each other and fear that they might lose what they had finally found.

The ache in her heart deepened, as it often did at night. Rather than give way to tears, she placed before her a little dream that she often nourished at bedtime, to take away the loneliness. It was an image of them all together again, sitting in the living room. After the war. Charles and the boys were gathered around her, looking down at the darling baby in her arms. A sweet little girl, named Charlotte, after Charles. Tommy and Gabriel were touching her tiny fingers, smiling at their little sister. And Charles – he looked from his daughter to her, and the tenderness in his eyes –

Tonight the vision didn't work, and her heart burst, taking her by surprise. There would be no more children; it would have happened by now. She had so badly wanted a child with Charles. She knew how happy it would make him. And her. But the war had come and forced them apart. And she was getting older. And Charles was so far away – she couldn't bear to think of him out there all alone. And what if – what if he – She pulled the pillow closer to her mouth, to muffle the sound of her crying.

Chapter 10

ᔓ

For the next several days, Ursula was careful to avoid Friedrich. She was a jumble of emotions, all getting in her way – not clear-headed, so unlike herself. Everything was changing so quickly. A year ago she was focused, and knew exactly what she wanted and how she was going to get it. Though she had postponed her plans for college when Paul enlisted, she continued to study on her own and had remained clear-sighted about what she wanted out of life.

But now? She was sure of nothing. She was behaving in a way that she had not thought possible – impetuous, impulsive, unsure of herself.

She hated that he thought so lowly of her – and she hated that she cared what he thought. He had called her a stupid girl, and he was right. Not for a moment had she considered that he might be able to speak other languages. Because she could speak only one language, she had assumed the same for him. She wanted him to know that she was going to college – after the war. She wanted to learn, to travel, to study other languages. A bit of Latin and French was all she had. She cringed at the memory of how she had freely insulted him for weeks, the hurtful words she had used.

But what did he mean about not calling him a Nazi? Weren't they all? How could she know? She was ignorant. But she wanted to know more. *No wonder he despises me. He has every right to.*

As she did every day, Ursula stood at her bedroom window, watching the pickup truck take away the prisoners. The setting sun gave the western sky a brief flush of pink, which soon disappeared and left the skies a heavy gray. She watched the truck leave the farm lane and turn onto the country road. When it was no longer in sight, she went downstairs to find Ed.

He was in the kitchen with Kate and Jessica, telling them how his wife was staying the night with her sister, who lived in the next town over, to help her with the holiday baking.

"Don't know what they can do, what with sugar so hard to come by these days. Opal says they'll cook with molasses and honey, add some raisins and other dried fruit. Every day she thanks you for the honey you sent. Puts it in her tea at breakfast. Says she's gotten to the point where she prefers it to sugar. Funny, how we get used to things."

"Why don't you stay for dinner, Ed?" said Kate, draining the water from the potatoes into the sink.

"She set me up with leftovers at home. Thanks, anyway."

"Let me set a plate for you, Ed," urged Ursula.

"And you don't want to miss out on Mom's fried chicken and mashed potatoes, do you?" asked Jessica.

Over dinner, the conversation settled on the POWs. They discussed how theirs compared to others at the surrounding farms, how much work they had accomplished in such a short time, and some of the cultural differences.

"First time we served them corn," said Ed, "they looked at it in surprise, then in confusion, wondering if it was some kind of joke or insult. They all looked up at Otto, who laughed heartily, and took a big spoonful of the buttery kernels. Then he said something to them all in German, and slowly they gave it a try. Otto said in Germany corn is used only for livestock." Ed chuckled at the memory. "Now, they can't get enough of it."

"Or my buttered cornbread," added Kate. She would never admit it, even to herself, but cooking for the POWs gave her a sense of satisfaction, as it had when she cooked for her sons. She loved nothing more than to see a hearty appetite become gratified by her cooking.

"Ed," asked Jessica, "why do they always sing? Have you noticed? Shirley said hers do the same thing, and Sue Ellen said Mr. Enchelmaier, their guard, says at camp they sing when they march, they sing when they work, they sing all the time."

Ed scratched his cheek, searching for an answer. "I guess it's just their way. Otto said Gustav told him that at the base camp they had an orchestra of sorts. Said that Friedrich has a beautiful voice, studied music at the university."

"That explains it," said Kate. "Once or twice he's been in the living room, and I wondered why he was staring so intently at the piano. I thought he was looking at the photographs on top. Perhaps he plays."

Ursula casually turned to Ed as she dished up some more potatoes. "Did Otto say that he majored in music?"

"No, that wasn't it." Ed rubbed his whiskers in thought. "Engineering, that's it. I knew it was something with machines."

"I hope the same three can help us in the spring," said Kate. "It would be a shame to have to start all over again. And we may not be so lucky the next time."

"Are they leaving?" asked Ursula, wondering if her voice had shown her alarm.

"Hard to say," said Ed. "The war's not ending any time soon, that's for sure. But Otto said the canneries up north are in need of labor. And once the cold weather sets in, I'm not sure how long we can keep 'em."

"Repairing the barn alone will take time," said Kate. "And I was hoping they could start on the outbuildings. They all have repairs that need done. And there are several trees that need cutting down. And if we have an early spring – "

Ed gave a low chuckle. "I know, Kate. We'll try to keep 'em. Lord knows, we can keep 'em busy."

"I hope they can stay. Or at least come back in the spring," said Jessica. "Shirley said her father sent one prisoner back. They just didn't like him, and the other prisoners always seemed tense when he was around – like he was spying on them. Mrs. Bloomfield was glad when he was gone."

"Ed," asked Ursula, "did Otto say anything about the prisoners not being Nazis?"

"You mean our prisoners?"

She moved her shoulder as if she didn't really care. "Just something I heard talked about in town. About some of the prisoners not being Nazis. I thought they all were."

"Oooh no," said Ed. "Otto said the three we have are all strongly anti-Nazi, though they keep it to themselves. Apparently, there are some POWs, maybe SS men, that the prisoners are afraid of."

"Maybe that's who was on the Bloomfield farm," said Jessica, her eyes wide with fear.

"Afraid how?" Kate asked Ed, passing him the platter of chicken.

"Well, 'reprisals back home,' is how Otto put it. Maybe here, as well. He said there was some trouble at the base camp where they came from."

"What do you mean – trouble?" asked Ursula.

"Well, apparently the Nazis pretty much control the camps, and have been allowed to keep some of their ways. Otto's brother works up north at Camp Ellis, and said the Nazi's keep order in the camps. Makes the guards' jobs a whole lot easier, especially since only a handful of guards speak German."

They all waited to see if Ed had more information to impart.

"Did our prisoners say anything about it?" asked Kate.

Ed rubbed his cheek. "Otto said all three of 'em requested farm work as a way to get out of the base camp. Now, this is all between ourselves – but they didn't like what was goin' on there."

"Like what?" asked Jessica.

"Otto said there were groups of hardcore Nazis who punished anyone who spoke out against Hitler."

"Punish how?" asked Ursula, suddenly afraid for Friedrich.

Ed clearly didn't want to say anything more. "Well," he said, rubbing his gray whiskers again, "best not to repeat things I can't know about."

*

The next day Ursula waited impatiently for Jessica to arrive home from school. She then convinced her to go with her to call on Shirley and Sue Ellen, to bring them some walnuts for their holiday baking. If any information were to be had, Mrs. Bloomfield was the person to ask. The tiniest prod would release any gossip she might have.

After a half hour of chatting at the Bloomfield table over tea and cookies, Sue Ellen steered the conversation to the Christmas dance at the Town Hall.

"Joe Madden finally got around to asking me. I knew he would. I don't know what took him so long. I had half a mind to tell Bart Eichen that I'd go with him."

"Go on," said Shirley. "Go show them your dress. It's beautiful."

Sue Ellen ran upstairs, delighted to have an excuse to try on her dress again.

"I'm still working on mine," said Shirley, "but let me show you." She ran to her room and came back with a dress made of the fabric she had chosen with Jessica back in October.

Jessica jumped up to look at the dress. "Oh, Shirley, it's so pretty! Mine's all finished. I added the trim around the neck, like you said. Ursula is going to wear her blue satin dress."

Ursula gave a quick look at Jessica, but didn't say anything.

Mrs. Bloomfield clapped her hands. "I'm so glad you're going, Ursula. Sue Ellen said you probably wouldn't, but I think it's very patriotic of you. We all must do our part for our boys. They'll all want to dance with you, I'm sure."

"Shirley! Come help!" Sue Ellen called from upstairs. "The sleeve is catching on a button or something. Come quick!"

Shirley and Jessica laughed and ran up the stairs to assist Sue Ellen.

Ursula made a show of trying to decide between the raisin bars and the oatmeal cookies. "Speaking of the war," she began, "Jessica said that you were glad to get rid of one of your POWs."

Mrs. Bloomfield gave a shudder. "I did not like that one from the beginning. A Nazi to the core. Didn't trust him one bit."

"I heard that some camps are having problems with the Nazis taking too much control. Do you know anything about that?"

"I do, indeed! Now, what I heard from Mrs. Pickett, the sheriff's wife, no less, is that those Nazis are bringing their devilish practices over here."

"What sort of – "

"She said that in some camps they've established a stronghold, still maintain their own rank and order, and if anyone doesn't agree – " she gave a knowing nod at the unfinished thought.

"What happens?"

Mrs. Bloomfield leaned forward, whispering. "If anyone speaks up, has anything good to say about America, or bad to say about Mr. Hitler, they get a visit at night from some ghastly group of thugs that calls itself – the Holy Ghost! Beatings mostly, though apparently some have resulted in death."

Ursula sat back in her chair, shocked at the information, and wondering if it was just a rumor. "I can't believe that would be allowed here in our own country."

"Oh, it's true, all right. It's all been hush hush – but the word is slowly getting out."

"Beatings by Nazis! While in prison here?" said Ursula, thinking of Friedrich.

"And worse," Mrs. Bloomfield added, shaking her head.

"Worse?" asked Ursula.

Again Mrs. Bloomfield leaned forward. "I don't want the younger girls to hear, but they say there have been *suicides*." She pursed her mouth and nodded. But seeing that Ursula wasn't following, she added, "Murders to look like suicides." She threw her hands up against the idea, and poured fresh tea into their cups.

Ursula felt sick to her stomach. The horrors of war were supposed to take place oceans away, not here at home. She thought of what Ed said about the POWs requesting farm work – and how Friedrich didn't know how to milk a cow. Her heart ached at the way she had treated him. Perhaps he had been in danger, and she had mocked him.

Mrs. Bloomfield patted Ursula's hand. "Why, you've gone quite pale! I didn't mean to upset you so. I figured you must have heard some of this from Otto." She pulled herself up to her stout-figured most. "Rest assured – they will *not* get away with such devilish behavior for much longer. We'll put a stop to their evil ways. You can be sure of that!" She turned and beamed at the vision of plump love-liness coming into the kitchen. "Oh, my heavens, Sue Ellen! You do look a picture! Doesn't she?"

Ursula suddenly found herself grateful for the fresh-faced wholesomeness of Sue Ellen, an antidote to the sickening information she had just heard. For a fleeting moment, she longed for their girlhood days, when their greatest concerns were where to find the best wild blackberries, or if they would win a ribbon at the fair.

She stood and admired Sue Ellen and her dress. "Just beautiful! That purple really suits you. You'll be the belle of the ball, Sue Ellen."

"Yes, I will!" Sue Ellen said, turning to admire her reflection in the hall mirror. "Just as long as *you* don't show up," she laughed good-naturedly.

*

The next day, Ursula made a jug of fresh coffee and cut up pieces of pumpkin bread and arranged them on a plate. She carried them out to the barn, where the prisoners were beginning on the repairs. Friedrich was up on a ladder and avoided looking at her, but came down when Otto called to him.

Ursula poured the coffee into their cups and made small talk with Otto and Ed, happy to see them all enjoying the unexpected treat. She waited for Friedrich to look up at her, but he took his coffee over to the barn entrance, and gazed out over the barren landscape.

While she waited for him to come back inside, she asked Otto about their progress and listened with interest as he explained the order of repairs, and how they would give them a fresh coat of paint when they were finished. She glanced over at Friedrich, but he remained looking out over the snow-dusted fields.

When Ursula left, she noticed something white in the straw at the base of the ladder. She pushed at it with her shoe, and lightly gasped. A photograph. Her heart beat faster. She knew she shouldn't look at it, but she couldn't stop herself.

She had to see it. She stooped to pick it up, turned it over, and on seeing the image, her face softened – a sweet young boy, no more than fourteen or fifteen, smiled up at the camera. Just as she held it closer, Friedrich snatched it out of her hand. Without looking at her, he put it in his shirt pocket. Avoiding her asking eyes, he walked back outside and began lifting and throwing lumber into the cart.

Karl walked up to Ursula and spoke gently. "*Sein jüngerer Bruder.*" He lowered his hand to indicate a lower height. "His brother. Killed at Stalingrad."

Chapter 11

~

Lillian's Saturday evening class was always more crowded and rowdier than the week-night classes – the patients stubbornly adhering to their pre-injury routine. Despite being boxed in by four walls, and newly limited by their wounded bodies, the men still craved the sense of celebration that only a Saturday night could bring – a way to end the week on a high note, before settling into the despair-laden tedium that began again on Sunday morning.

Tonight Lillian herself was in a more buoyant mood, excited about her evening out with Izzy and Archie. She glanced at the clock, expecting Izzy at any moment, but she decided not to say anything to the men about her visit.

"I forget how you said to use the brush," Sergeant Remling said, who, at the last class, had ambitiously asked for painting materials. He made room beside him for Lillian.

She leaned on the table across from him and demonstrated.

"Like this?" he asked.

"No," Lillian said. She moved to the other side and patiently guided his hand. "Like this," she said, once again showing him how to hold the brush, how to move his wrist. "Lightly, allow it to flow. That's right." She guided his hand until he was able to copy the fluid movement on his own, which caused the others to laugh.

"Watch out for Rembrandt, Miss Lillian," teased Memphis. "That leg of his is almost healed."

Lillian straightened up and addressed the men who were laughing. "At least he's serious about his lessons. He's going to surprise his mother with a drawing before he gets out of here, aren't you?"

Remling bobbed his head up and down eagerly, which made the men laugh all the more.

Lillian gave a playful look of reprimand to the group. "You could all do the same, if you would just apply yourselves a little more."

Remling smiled at the praise and held up his latest depiction of Lillian, which was not much of an improvement from his first attempt. He didn't seem to mind that it brought about more loud guffaws, and he good-naturedly laughed along with the others.

"No one applies himself like Rembrandt," said Mack, setting off a new round of laughter.

"Come show *me* how to hold my brush. Maybe I can get the same results," said another.

Lillian had learned that the best way to discourage their insinuating remarks was to simply ignore them.

"If you don't practice in between lessons, then it doesn't matter what I teach you," she responded.

The young GI clutched his heart. "Aw, you're breakin' my heart, Teacher. I just need a little private time with you."

"It's my turn Rembrandt," said Bushwick. "Stop hoggin' all the time."

"I'm not hogging all the time, but I have to work on my *technique*."

"We all know what technique that would be." Bushwick pushed Remling aside and grabbed his paint brush. "I know what game you're playing."

"You don't know up from down, you dumb Dago."

"Hey, who you callin' a dumb Dago?" Rossi challenged, eager to get in on the fray.

Several other patients elbowed their way forward, adding a fresh round of taunts. Though Lillian tried to quell the growing squabble, it soon escalated into a fracas with more imaginative insults being hurled about, along with the tossing of wadded-up drawings, raised voices, a great deal of laughter and –

As if a magic wand were waved over the room, the men froze into position – mouths open, arms poised above their heads in a toss, a crutch pointed like a weapon, an elbow ready to rib the guy nearby.

The room filled with silence, broken only by a long slow whistle from one of the men.

Izzy stood in the doorway.

"Hello, boys!" Izzy looked out at the disorderly scene. "This must be the drawing class." She slung her coat over one shoulder and held a covered basket in her other hand. Her deep green hat sat angled in her auburn curls.

"I came to bring you a little holiday cheer," she said. She walked into the room, her red dress shimmering with movement.

The men remained immobile, puzzling out if her tone was seductive or innocent.

Then, as if to dispel their confusion, but in fact, compounding it, she set the basket down on the table, and dramatically whipped off the cloth – revealing a platter brimming with Christmas cookies. Her body language conveyed one message, the cookies another. She gave Lillian a quick wink as she draped her coat over the back of the chair and set her hat on top of it. Then she slowly smoothed down her dress over her hips, raised her face to the roomful of men, and gave them one of her dazzling smiles.

A flurry of activity followed, wheelchairs were wheeled closer to the table, the card game in the back broke up, and the men moved forward to the table where Lillian was trying to introduce Izzy.

"This is my friend, Izzy Briggs, that I was telling you about." Lillian raised her voice above the questions and comments coming from all directions. "She's graciously agreed to model for you so that – Tonight we're going to learn – " but she was interrupted left and right. She gave up and tried to make a few individual introductions. "This is Private Rossi, and this – "

"Introduce me to your friend!" said Remling, planting himself next to Izzy.

"This is Sergeant Rembrandt – I mean Remmy – I mean – " Lillian grew increasingly flustered as the class spun out of control. "And over here is – "

But the men had all pushed forward on their own, shaking Izzy's hand, and telling her their names.

Izzy quickly took command.

With hands on her hips, she raised her voice. "Okay, boys, get out your materials, and let's get started." She raised her head to the back of the room. "Is that music I hear?"

"Yes, ma'am," answered one of the younger men from the back. "Do you want me to turn it down?"

"No! Turn it up! That's Benny Goodman!" and she took the hands of a GI in a wheelchair, his face brightening as he fell right in with her moves.

The atmosphere changed as Izzy stepped about the room, greeting the men, while Lillian attempted to conduct the class. "Okay, get into your groups – We'll begin with a series of five-minute sketches – or maybe two-minute sketches."

Lillian tried to help Izzy hold a position, which didn't last long, with the men introducing themselves and asking her questions. But some of the more earnest students were eagerly trying to capture her face, her expressions – others focused on her gestures, her figure.

Izzy turned down the various invitations, explaining that she had a certain sergeant filling her life at the moment. Then she tossed her head back in laughter at a witty remark from one GI, and had a ready comeback for another. A few Santa hats got tossed around from man to man, with Izzy intercepting one, and putting it on.

Lillian passed around the cookie basket while Izzy struck poses: sitting on the table with her legs crossed, then on the lap of one GI, and then with her arms looped around another. A few men danced with Izzy or spun her around as she passed by. Izzy included all the men, refusing to see crutches or wheelchairs as obstacles. She placed a sympathetic hand on their shoulders, and in a few seconds found out where they from, if they had family. It became an impromptu Christmas party, with more men from the hall stopping in and participating.

At one point, Lillian gave up trying to teach, and simply watched her friend. She knew that Izzy had the ability to turn on the charm and had often seen her in action. But this was different.

Though it all appeared spontaneous, Izzy was making sure to address every single man, spending equal time with each patient, and maintaining absolute control over the degree of flirtation. She encouraged a certain amount, let it brim to a point, and then reeled it back in. She matched the serious tone in a few of the men, and with the younger ones she became ten years younger in an instant.

There she was, joking with the men, making them laugh, making them all feel special. It was a kind of unstudied performance – inclusive, playful, and yet sincere. She flirted with joy, in a wholesome, pleasant manner. The older men seemed to smile in memory, the younger ones in hope of some future dream.

Lillian studied the men's faces and realized that they had changed – they were different tonight – no longer patients. Izzy, with her infectious charm, had made each of them feel like "men."

Lillian looked around at the different faces and caught a glimpse of what the men were like before they were wounded, before the war had burdened them with pain and struggle and an uncertain future.

The time flew by, and Lillian was surprised when one of the nurses poked her head in the door and held up five fingers to indicate that some of the men would soon have to take their medicines or treatment.

Lillian was reluctant to call time, but they had already exceeded the class by half an hour.

"Okay, our time is up. Let's look at your results."

Amid groans and protestations, the men finally gave in, and Lillian and Izzy moved about the room, examining the drawings. Many pages remained blank or had only a few lines drawn, but other students had done their best to capture the essence of Izzy – in all of the drawings she was smiling.

The group of patients clearly didn't want the party to end and did their best to prolong it with requests for Izzy to visit again.

"You gotta come back, Izzy!"

"I didn't get a chance to finish my drawing!"

"I'll be waiting for you, Miss Izzy!"

Izzy slipped on her coat and adjusted her hat. "I promise to come back – but only if you promise to improve on these chicken scratches!" She held up one drawing of a lumpy woman in red and gasped. Then she ran her hand over her hair and batted her eyes. "I do hope I look better than this!"

As she made her way to the door, the crowd followed, including the men on crutches and in wheelchairs.

"Okay, boys," she said, her palm raised to signal the end. "I'm afraid duty calls and I must offer my," she gave a discreet little cough behind the back of her hand, "talents, elsewhere" – which caused a new outburst of laughter and whistles.

Izzy leaned into Lillian. "See you soon?"

Lillian nodded, squeezed her friend's hand, and whispered, "Thank you!"

Amid such parting remarks as "have a drink on me!" and "tell that sergeant he doesn't know how lucky he is," and "if things don't work out with him . . .," Izzy backed out of the door, blowing them all a big kiss.

For a moment the room fell silent.

Then Remling asked, "You got any more friends like that?" and the buzz started up again, the men ribbing one another and telling tales about who she reminded them of, and a girl someone met at . . ., and another with the figure like . . .

"And on that note," said Lillian, packing up her supplies, "I think I'll take my leave."

There were a few "my heart still belongs to you," and the like.

Lillian laughed and said goodbye, passing the coordinator in the hall. Lillian was afraid that she might be reprimanded for allowing the class to turn into a party.

But Mrs. Coppel simply gave a light chuckle. "If laughter is the best medicine, then those men just got a heavy dose of it."

Lillian smiled at the comment, and then went upstairs to see her private students.

She was still flushed with the excitement of the impromptu party. Her eyes were bright and her smile wide as she sat down next to her youngest student. After the first few classes, she had insisted that all the students address her on a first name basis.

"Good evening, Ernest," she said somewhat breathless from her rush. "I hope I haven't kept you waiting." She noticed that he was sitting up in bed with a worried expression.

"I was afraid you weren't coming."

"Tonight's class ran a little longer than usual." She patted his hand and he quickly grasped it. "What is it, Ernest? Is anything wrong?"

She glanced over at her other student, Mr. Carmichael, but saw that he was in a deep sleep, and returned her attention to Ernest.

"I might not get another chance," Ernest said. "There's something I – I have to get something off my chest."

Little alarm bells went off in Lillian, but the pleading sweetness in his face made her sympathetic to whatever he had to say.

"I – I love you, Lillian. I can't help it, but I do. You have to believe me."

Lillian sat back in her chair, struck silent by his confession. Then she smiled and leaned forward. "Ernest, I do believe you. But what you feel isn't – that kind of love. There are all kinds of love, and in a way, I have come to love you, and all my students."

"No, you don't understand. When I'm with you, I feel better, stronger, happier. And I know that I'm going to get out of here – and live again."

"Well, that's a good thing. And that's why I'm here – to help you all as you reconnect with life. But that's a different kind of love."

His face flooded with boyish disappointment that she wasn't taking him seriously.

"Ernest. Not only am I already married, but I'm old enough to be your mother."

He blinked in disbelief. "You are?"

"Yes," she laughed. "I have a son not much younger than you – perhaps five years or so."

"You do?" He pulled his head back and looked closely at her, seeing her in a new light.

Lillian nodded.

"Gee, that's hard to believe."

"I think when you're up and about again you'll see that what you feel for me is a kind of appreciation, like you feel for Nurse Ellen and Doctor Carter."

He looked away and slowly nodded. Then he quickly looked up at her again, as if wondering how she could have aged so quickly.

"Right now, we're your world and it's natural for you to grow attached to us, just as we've grown attached to you. But soon you'll be mixing with people your own age and seeing things differently – though it seems to me there are a few young people around who would be quite happy for your company." She smiled over at one of the Red Cross volunteers.

When Ernest looked up to see what she meant, Lillian gently pointed her chin to the pretty young girl, who quickly smiled and then turned away.

"I never really noticed her before."

"That's because she's shy. But she's noticed you."

Ernest observed the young woman as she moved about the room.

"Nurse Ellen tells me that she's one of the best assistants here, and that she wants to become a nurse. Though dating the patients is prohibited, perhaps you could show her your work. She's asked me, on more than one occasion, what you liked to draw."

"She did?" Again, he looked over at the young volunteer.

Lillian nodded. She then lifted his notebook and flipped through his drawings. "You're very good, Ernest. I really think you should continue with classes when you're up to it. In the meantime, just keep practicing."

They spent a few minutes going over his drawings, with Lillian making suggestions and pointing out his progress.

Ernest smiled at her remarks. "It's really helped me, having these classes. You'll still stop by, won't you? Until I leave?"

"Of course, I will. Though Dr. Carter said he thinks you'll be able to leave before Christmas."

He smiled and his face finally took on the glow of hope. "My family's counting on it." He was soon talking about his plans for Christmas, and read out parts of his letters to her. Every now and then, he glanced over at the shy Red Cross volunteer.

Lillian spent another twenty minutes with Mr. Carmichael, who had just woken up. She then left the ward, and went down to the coordinator's office, where she returned her smock. She stood in front of the mirror on the wall and brushed her hair and powdered her nose.

Mrs. Coppel came in with a clipboard in hand, followed by two new volunteers. She stopped and gaped at Lillian in her lustrous green dress.

"Oh, Mrs. Drooms! You look beautiful!"

"Thank you, Mrs. Coppel. I rarely go out, but tonight I'm making an exception."

"Well, we all need a little cheer in these dark times. You have yourself a wonderful evening." She picked up a large folder from her desk, and left the room with the volunteers hurrying behind her.

Lillian glanced at her reflection. She was wearing her favorite dress – a deep green satin and chiffon that seemed perfect for the holidays – even though it was too long for the fashion of the day. Hemlines had crept up to the knee in order to save on fabric, and though she had a few newer dresses, this one was special to her.

It was the dress she had worn the first time she and Charles went out – over three years ago now. It reminded her of him, of them, of their time together, and she had hesitated before deciding to wear it. But his recent letter had convinced her to try to go out and enjoy herself, and so she had worn it, in part, to feel closer to Charles. And now she was glad she had listened to him. She was really looking forward to the evening. To meeting Izzy's beau, to being around people in the holiday spirit, to seeing what other women were wearing in these times of restrictions.

She took her clip earrings out of her purse, clusters of small crystals that picked up on the emerald of her dress, and smoothed on a brighter shade of lipstick. Then she took a final look in the mirror, expecting to feel the same sense of glamor she had felt going out with Charles – but instead of excitement, a sense of loss washed over her, that Charles was not there with her. She could almost see him in the mirror, standing just behind her, his hand on her shoulder, that look of love and tender-ness in his eyes.

She shook away the sadness and determined to be cheerful. After all, it was Christmas. She was meeting Izzy and – her fiancé? She could hardly believe it. Fresh under the cheerful influence of Izzy, Lillian straightened her shoulders and smiled. She *would* have a wonderful time.

By the time she arrived at the club, it was late – for her. Ten o'clock. The mood in the club had that late-night party feel; swing music filled the air, everyone moved to the music, all happy and hopeful.

Lillian realized that she hadn't been in such a gathering for years. The sense of excitement, of participating in the flow of life, filled her once again. She held her head high and smiled out at the crowded room. The pillars and ceiling were festooned with holiday streamers and small red poinsettias sat in the middle of the tables. Most of the men were dressed in military white, navy, or olive drab, and the women sparkled in their holiday attire. Sheer exuberance pervaded the air like a heady fragrance.

There was Izzy on the dance floor, dancing cheek to cheek with her beau. When the couple spun around, Lillian's smile dropped – and for a dizzying moment, Lillian thought she was seeing things. It was as if she were looking back into the past, seeing Izzy dance with Red. Then she caught a better glimpse of him – not Red, but there were some startling similarities. Archie was almost as tall as Red, had the same sandy red hair, and was handsome – but altogether different, as well. More boyish, fresh-faced.

Izzy waved when she spotted Lillian and began to pull Archie over to her.

"Lilly!" Izzy wove her way over to Lillian and embraced her giddily. "This is Sergeant Archibald Reynolds! Archie."

Lillian smiled at the flushed couple and tried to make herself heard over the music. "Hello, Archie! So nice to finally meet you."

"So you're Lillian!" He gave a wide smile and clasped her hand. "I've heard a lot about you – couldn't wait to meet you."

"Over here! Follow me," said Izzy, pulling Archie behind her. They threaded their way single file to their table, where two other couples were sitting. They squeezed in and Izzy briefly introduced Lillian to them and to a few people at the table next to them. There was a lot of coming and going, the people at the two tables switching places as they came and went onto the dance floor.

Archie soon had drinks ordered for them, and began talking over the music to tell Lillian about how he met Izzy in the spring, and how they were spending their time together.

Lillian was taken with his charm and could understand why Izzy had fallen for him. He was friendly, open, and good-natured, all smiles and enthusiasm.

Izzy tugged on his sleeve. "Red, snag the waitress and ask – " She smacked her head at her slip of the tongue.

Archie smiled and shrugged. "She does that all the time," he laughed. "I told her I'm not going to propose until she gets my name right."

Lillian glanced at Izzy, but she was oblivious to Lillian's look of concern.

Izzy was in her element, now – pairing men and women with each other, introducing people who were just joining the table, laughing, her arm around Archie, dancing with him and the other men at the tables who cut in or came to ask her to dance.

An officer from the other table returned to his seat, and was soon introduced to Lillian as Corporal Donald Conway.

"Please. Call me Don – we're all friends here. So you know Izzy? I haven't seen you here before."

A conversation soon began, followed by a turn around the dance floor. Now and then another man would cut in and dance with her, but somehow Corporal Conway managed to end the dance and escort her back to the table. He asked all about her, and Lillian found herself talking about Charles and the boys. She reciprocated by asking him about his family and his plans for the holiday – and was somewhat surprised that such a handsome man was still unmarried.

When she returned to the table after a few dances, Izzy took her arm and dragged her to the powder room. Lillian knew Izzy would ask what she thought about Archie and was unsure how to respond.

"Watch out for that one," said Izzy, gesturing to Corporal Conway who was dancing with a woman from the table next to theirs. "Don Conway – also known as Don Juan. I've heard rumors about him. A real seducer."

"Oh, Izzy. You think that about all men. He's been the perfect gentleman."

"So far," said Izzy. "The night's young."

Lillian shook her head at Izzy's insinuations.

Inside the powder room, Izzy was unable to contain her excitement. "Well? What do you think? Isn't Archie just perfect?"

"He's very nice," said Lillian, looking in the mirror as she applied some lipstick and then blotted it.

Izzy's face fell. "Well, that's a helluva way to praise someone."

"No, I mean it. He's charming and funny." Lillian looked at Izzy in the mirror and saw her disappointment.

"I was so sure you were going to love him."

"He's wonderful, Izzy. He's a real gem. Anyone can see that."

Izzy crossed her arms and leaned against the counter. "But what?"

"It's just that – I didn't expect him to remind me so much of Red."

Izzy laughed with relief. "Is that all? That's just a coincidence."

Lillian didn't want to burst Izzy's happiness; she nodded and smiled, ready to go back out.

But Izzy held up her hand. "Oh no, you don't. I know when something's on your mind."

"It doesn't matter what I think. Let's just have fun tonight." Lillian smiled and put on her happiest face. Which didn't fool Izzy at all.

"Tell me what you're thinking."

Lillian looked down, unsure how to phrase what she was feeling. "Well – it's as if you're reliving your time with Red. You go to the same places. Several times you even referred to Archie as Red."

"Just a slip of the tongue. I'm wild about this guy."

"Are you sure, Izzy? Are you sure it's Archie you're enamored with? Or is it the memory of Red?"

"That's ridiculous! Archie's the real thing. And if he asks me to marry him, I'm going to say yes!" Izzy raised her chin, ready to refute any possible objection Lillian might raise.

"Do you love him?"

Izzy opened her mouth, but was unable to answer. A fleeting hint of sadness filled her eyes. Then she spun around and left in a huff.

"Izzy, wait!" Lillian tried to catch up to her, but as soon as they got to the table, Archie pulled Izzy out onto the dance floor.

Lillian was soon dancing again with Corporal Conway, and when they brushed by Archie and Izzy, Lillian saw that she was all smiles again. She was familiar with Izzy's temporary flare ups, but still, she promised herself not to say anything else about Archie. What did she know? Everything these days was all confused and desperate and fragmented. She wanted Izzy to be happy. And she wanted to enjoy herself, wanted to be part of the Christmas festivity.

The lights and gaiety, drinks and dancing, made Lillian more talkative than usual. She found herself enjoying the evening, speaking alternately with Donald Conway, Izzy and Archie, and the other people who came and went. When one of the women asked Lillian about her work with Rockwell Publishing, a conversation soon began on painting, which was quickly taken up by Corporal Conway.

"My sister, Sally, is a painter – mostly self-taught, but she wants to pursue a degree in art." He asked Lillian her opinion about what course of action to take to secure a job in the art field, and what her plans were for her own career.

Lillian grew enthusiastic as she gave information to encourage his sister, and then revealed her plans to someday become a freelance illustrator. She noticed that one of the women at the next table, who danced now and then with Donald, was observing her. The woman looked on with an amused smile, more of a smirk. Lillian glanced over at the woman now and then, wondering what she meant.

But Donald soon pulled Lillian onto the dance floor, and when the music shifted to a slow number, he convinced her to stay and dance with him. Once or twice, she thought his hand had too intimately stroked her back, her waist, but whenever she looked at him, he was smiling, all courtesy and gentlemanly behavior.

The dance floor was growing more and more crowded, and they were often pressed close together.

Lillian began to feel uncomfortable. She had never been at ease in crowds, and the boisterousness seemed to increase with the lateness of the hour.

Donald pulled Lillian nearer to him, protecting her from the jostling crowd. His mouth was close to her ear in order to be heard. She thought he said something about getting away – and with a start, she leaned back and looked up at him. But he was saying what a handsome couple Izzy and Archie made, and she assumed she had misunderstood him.

He smiled warmly and his hand slid down to her lower back.

She pushed back from him a little. "I – I feel too warm."

"I can help with that," he said, smiling. He began to lead her away, and she had to admit that she was relieved to get away from the pressing crowd.

"Come. It's cooler over here." He led her to the bar, and helped her to a seat, while he ordered more drinks.

"I think I'll just have water. I'm so thirsty," Lillian said, fanning herself with her hand. "It was too close out there."

"I agree." He paid for their drinks, and handed her one. "This will cool you down until I can get you some water."

"Thank you." She sipped the drink and looked around for Izzy. She soon spotted her on the dance floor. Izzy waved at her and then leaned her cheek against Archie's. Lillian smiled, thankful that Izzy hadn't stayed angry.

Donald leaned into her and placed an arm snug around her waist.

Lillian was taken aback by the freedom he was taking, and removed his arm. Perhaps he had had too much to drink. She would return to the table. Say goodnight to Izzy, and leave.

Donald put his mouth to her ear and spoke in a voice full of expectation. "Why don't you finish that and come with me. My hotel is close by. We'll go there for a night cap."

Lillian's head snapped up. "Excuse me?"

"I can tell you want to – as badly as I do. You're a beautiful woman, Lillian. I'd like to show you how I treat beautiful women."

Lillian's stomach flipped in disgust. She sat up straight and spoke with as much control as she could muster. "I think we've misjudged one another."

She reached for her clutch and began to push off from the bar stool, but he put his arm around her, surrounding her with his body. She could feel the heat and strength and desire pouring off of him.

"Hey, no need to be offended," he said softly. "You wouldn't be the first wife to find comfort while her husband's away. It's to be expected."

"How dare you!" she said, eyes ablaze.

But he was not to be so easily put off. "Come on, you don't have to play coy with me. I know what you want." He leaned into her, his husky voice in her hair. "You're so lonely and hungry I can smell it."

Lillian pushed him back, and stood, her eyes flashing with anger – which only seemed to amuse him, and his smile widened. In her mind she slapped him sharply – and yet it was her own cheek that burned red.

He stood there smiling, expectant – and utterly repulsive.

She left the bar, and made her way to the Ladies room, trembling with indignation. Once inside, she took out her powder and tried to tone down the flush in her cheeks.

The smirking woman from the table soon followed her in. She wore a tight-fitting, gold-lamé dress and she slouched against the counter. After slowly pulling a cigarette case from her purse, she took out a cigarette, and tapped it on the case, all the while staring at Lillian.

Lillian looked up at her, wondering if she was somehow in on it.

"I told him not to try with you – that you were too high-minded for him. It's written all over you – an old-fashioned kind of girl. But that just whetted his appetite all the more."

"Who are you?" Lillian asked, repulsed by the woman and her orange lipstick and stiff blonde hair.

The woman looked up and down Lillian. "I hope you didn't fall for the line about his sister Sally." There was that smirk again.

Lillian grabbed her clutch. As she opened the door to leave, the woman called out, snickering. "He doesn't even have a sister!"

Her laughter seemed to follow Lillian as she made her way to the coat check. The beating of the music and the playful melody was at odds with her sense of shame and disgust as she waited for her coat. She slipped it on, and quickly left the club.

Lillian welcomed the slap of cold air as she pushed open the door and rushed out into the night. How dare he! What had she been thinking – why had she thought he was a gentleman? No one had *ever* spoken to her like that – with such crude desire and presumption.

She put her hand to her mouth and began walking, almost running, just away. Away from everything. She stepped out into the street and flagged down a taxi, causing it to swerve to a stop.

All during the ride home, she blamed herself for being so foolish, so naïve. He was nothing better than a rake! And that horrible woman. How disgusting! She hated them both. Why had she even gone out? She would have been better off staying at home. Knitting.

She paid hurriedly, ran up the stairs to her apartment, and closed the door behind her, still trembling in outrage. She felt as if she had betrayed Charles. How could she have been so stupid? She threw down her coat and hat, and ran a hot bath, but the anger and sense of shame was slow to leave her. Izzy had tried to warn her, but she thought she knew better.

Nothing is clear anymore, she thought. Everything is crumbling, everyone is so desperate – grasping at each other in their frenzied hunger. It was all so disorienting. Had she done anything to encourage his behavior? She suddenly remembered Ernest and his declaration of love just a few hours earlier. Was she perhaps unwittingly putting out some signal? Could everyone see something that she could not?

No. Only she knew her heart. Only she knew how much she loved Charles. He was the only man on earth for her. If she had committed any mistake, it was in imaging him there with her. She had felt him with her all night, imagined his eyes on her, his hand on her shoulder.

She stepped out of the bath, feeling that she had washed the night off of her, and slipped on a nightgown. But when she looked at the empty bed, she sank to her knees, her arms outstretched on the bed – glad that the boys were gone so that she could freely give in to her wretchedness. She was unspeakably lonely. She called Charles's name again and again, the sound of his name causing her skin to tingle with desire and sadness all mixed up together, overwhelmed at the emptiness she felt without him. Never had she felt so hopelessly hungry for his voice, his arms around her, his mouth on hers. And all she could do was cry with longing and misery. Fighting against the fear, what if – what if he didn't come back to her? What if – he didn't survive the war? She couldn't bear it.

She buried her face in her hands, and then frustrated at her weakness, she pushed off from the bed and went to the closet. She fumbled through his shirts, searching for any lingering trace of him, his cologne. Then she slipped off her nightgown, and put on one of his shirts. She wanted him desperately, missed him, didn't know how to fill the aching void. If just once more she could hold him, breathe him in, bury herself in him.

Then the lines from his letter came to her: *Every night I look out across the black ocean and know that you are there.*

She went to the window, raised it, and looked out into the darkness, to wherever he was. From some faraway shore, was he trying to feel her, as desperately lonely for her as she was for him?

The cold wind blew over her, chilling her, calming the fire in her blood. She peered through the night, beyond the city lights, over the dark ocean, to the place where her beloved stood and looked her way. Out into the frigid wild air, she sent her love, her words – and as the tears grew cold on her cheeks, she closed her eyes, and felt his lips on hers. And it was real. It was not just desire and dreaming. He was with her, pressing his warm lips on hers.

Never had she felt so connected to him; and she knew that nothing would ever come between them. They were one thing now, not two separate people. And the knowledge of that made her strong.

She would make it through the war, would make it through the loneliness, would make it through whatever came, whatever happened. For nothing was stronger than love. She raised her chin to the cold dark night, and gently smiled – full, powerful, strong.

Chapter 12

In the late afternoon, Jessica stood at the window, her eyes fixed on the road at the end of the lane.

"They're here!" she cried, waving at the old Pontiac that was turning onto the farm lane. "Mom! The Bloomfields are here!"

"All right, all right," said Kate, setting the last of the pies onto the table. For the past two days, she and her daughters had baked apple, pumpkin, and pecan pies for the Christmas dance, and Jessica had proudly put the finishing touches on her gingerbread house.

Kate glanced over at her younger daughter, pleased that she was so excited. All week Jessica had been giddy with anticipation, talking about who was baking what dessert, what items were going to be raffled, and which boys from school she wanted to dance with.

Jessica was dressed in her red and black plaid dress that she had made in November in anticipation of the dance. Her hair was curled and set off with a black velvet ribbon. And, if Kate wasn't mistaken, there was a bit of color added to her lips. Ah well, she thought, let Jessica have her fun tonight. There was so little in the way of amusement for her daughters that she was happy the dance was going to be such a big event. Life on the farm could be lonely at times. And tonight folks from all the towns around would be there, offering a chance to catch up and hear what news and gossip everyone had. Kate was looking forward to seeing her old friend Rachel and her family, and some cousins from an hour away that she hadn't seen since summer.

There was Jessica, all bright and pretty, and Ursula would wear her blue dress that so set off her coloring. Kate was proud of her daughters and was happy that everyone would get a chance to see how lovely they were becoming.

Kate inspected her reflection in the mirror. Not bad for being in her fifties, she thought, smoothing down her burgundy crepe dress. She adjusted the poinsettia brooch her husband had given her – goodness, it must be twenty years ago. Her dark hair was streaked with gray, and though she had her doubts, Ursula insisted that it added a touch of elegance.

Jessica stood in the doorway waiting for Shirley, who had stopped to chat with Ed, Otto, and the prisoners out in the farmyard.

Mrs. Bloomfield eased herself out of the car and made her way to the group. "Evenin'!" she said to Otto. She glanced up at the late afternoon sky. "Well, almost, anyway. *Gutten dag*, to you two," she said to Karl and Gustav.

They smiled and nodded to her. Friedrich watched from the barn where he was finishing up painting the repairs.

"You coming to the dance, Otto? You have to come," said Shirley. "We'll be selling raffle tickets and if you're lucky, you just might win my date nut bread or Sue Ellen's famous apple strudel."

"Or my gingerbread house," said Jessica, joining her friend.

"Just wait'll you see it!" said Shirley. "A gingerbread house complete with snowdrifts, a snowman, and gum-drop trees."

"Oh, I'll be there, all right. I wouldn't miss it for the world," said Otto. "Zack's still down with bronchitis, so I'll be pickin' up the boys at the other farms and takin' them back to camp. But I'll be there in time for dinner, you can count on that!" He hooked his thumbs behind his overall straps and turned to Ed. "You'll be there, won't you Ed?"

"Indeed, he will!" Mrs. Bloomfield answered for him. "Opal's in charge of the dessert table and needs his help. I hear tell the hall's already filling up – and dinner doesn't start for another hour."

Ed smiled and nodded. "I'll drop off Kate and Ursula, then I'll go home and change. We'll be right behind you all."

"Evenin'!" Mrs. Bloomfield called to Kate, who now stood on the porch with the door open.

"Do you have time for a cup of coffee?" asked Kate.

"Heavens no!" Mrs. Bloomfield answered, hoisting herself up the stairs to the porch. "Orville is already in a stitch that he has to wear a suit for tonight. The sooner I get him to the hall, and get some food in his stomach, the better for us all," she laughed. "I just came to help with the desserts."

She made her way into the kitchen, and gasped with pleasure on seeing five assorted pies laid out on the table. "Look at those! No one bakes a pie like you, Kate. Make sure I get a piece of that one," she said, admiring the pecan pie.

Kate beamed at the compliment, and took out two baskets from the pantry and set them on the kitchen table. Mrs. Bloomfield gently placed two pies in each of the baskets, while Kate stepped over to the stairs.

"Ursula!" she called. "Come down. We need your help!" She came back to the kitchen and put an arm around Jessica and Shirley. "You girls can take the baskets, and I'll carry the gingerbread house to the car. I'll set it between you two, and, for heaven's sake, make sure it doesn't fall."

"No chance of that," said Jessica. "Not after it took me so long to make."

Amid all the commotion, Otto directed Friedrich and Karl to set some of the paint supplies just outside the kitchen door on the back porch. Karl was talking cheerfully to Otto, observing the bustle in the kitchen.

Friedrich set down a paint can, and when he looked up he saw Ursula walk into the kitchen, wearing the blue dress.

She stopped suddenly on seeing him there.

He tried to look away, but he couldn't take his eyes off her. She stood framed in the doorway, the light from the living room illuminating her hair. A shadow of pain filled his face, as if his heart would break – he had never seen anything lovelier. He couldn't look away.

Ursula hadn't expected to see him. She stared back, unable to move, while her hands clenched the fabric at the sides of her dress.

"Ursula," said Kate. "Don't just stand there – go and get the box for the gingerbread house." Then seeing Friedrich and Karl, Kate asked them, "How about a cup of coffee to warm you up before you leave? Coffee?" she asked loudly, mimicking drinking a cup.

"*Nein, danke,*" they said, shaking their heads. Karl grinned widely, enjoying the preparation for the festivities. Friedrich said something in German to Karl, and went back out to the barn.

Kate set the gingerbread house into the box Ursula had set on the table, and surrounded it with some cotton batting. She made a few adjustments to keep it from shifting, and then she gently lifted the box.

"I'll carry the pecan pie," said Mrs. Bloomfield. "Ursula, dear, can you open the door? My, but you do look lovely!"

Ursula smiled and held the door open for them. She watched as they carefully walked to the car, fearful of slipping and ruining all their hard work. She glanced over at the barn. Friedrich had been watching her, but turned away when she saw him, and went inside the barn.

Kate greeted the uncomfortable looking Mr. Bloomfield, and set the box in the middle of the back seat. Once the girls were settled, she closed the car door.

"We'll be right behind you!" she hollered, waving goodbye.

Ed and Otto touched their hats in goodbye, and then Otto went back into the barn.

Ed took a moment to look around at the farmyard, all quiet now. He took off his hat, smoothed his hair, and adjusted the hat back on his head, feeling a little younger and eager to be standing with his wife at the dessert table as they had done for the past several years. He smiled to know that she would be there waiting for him. They would make sure everyone had their dessert, then they would have their dinner and watch the young folk dance. He gave a little chuckle knowing that he, too, would take a spin or two around the floor. After all, his wife was still the best dancer in town. He gave a final glance around the farmyard, and returned to the kitchen to fetch Kate and Ursula.

Kate gave a sigh of relief, happy that the pies and gingerbread house were safely on their way to the hall. She put on her coat and hat, glancing periodically at the stairs for Ursula to come back down. Then she lifted her purse and gloves.

She glanced at the clock. "Ursula! We have to help set up." She put one hand on the banister and called up the stairs. "I thought you were all ready."

All day Kate had kept an eye on Ursula. Something was not right. She had missed dinner more than once this past week, saying she was tired. She was often distracted, often gazed out of the windows, or looked out into the farmyard. Kate didn't know what to make of the girl; but now was not the time to worry about it. They were going to be late if they didn't hurry.

Ed came into the kitchen. "Otto and the boys are just finishing up – be another half hour or so. I'll go get the truck and pull up in front."

"That's fine," said Kate. "I'll leave the kitchen light on in case they need anything." She looked around, growing impatient. "Ursula! We're ready to leave – get your coat."

She was just about to call again, when Ursula came into the kitchen, looking pale and distraught.

"What is it?" asked Kate, putting her hand on her daughter's forehead. "Don't you feel well? I was afraid you were getting sick."

"I'm fine. I just – I just don't feel up to the dance. I'm sorry, but – I'm just tired."

Kate's face fell in disappointment for her daughter. "It's the big dance of the season – are you sure you want to miss it? We could leave early. We don't have to wait for the Bloomfields. Ed would be happy to give us a lift back when you want."

"No. Please. I – I really don't want to go."

"You'll be disappointing the boys – some of them home on leave. They'll all be asking about you."

"I know, but – I can't. I just – can't."

Kate put her arm around her daughter's shoulder. "Do you want me to stay with you?"

"No. You have to go. And besides," Ursula added with a forced smile, "I'll want to hear all about it, and your version will be much more accurate than Jessica's. I'm fine, really. I think I'll just sleep for a bit."

Kate saw the dark circles under her daughter's eyes and the pale cheeks. "All right then. Go lie down. Maybe a rest is what you need. But make sure you have some dinner when you wake up."

Kate slipped on her gloves and saw that Ed had driven the pickup truck around to the front porch. "I'll bring you back a piece of Sue Ellen's famous apple strudel."

Ursula gave a small laugh. "I'll be waiting up for it." She watched her mother get into the truck and drive off, and then she closed the door. The house was strangely quiet after the bustling activity of the last few days. She welcomed the silence as she climbed the stairs back to her room.

She stood at her window and gazed out over the late afternoon fields. The stubble of the corn fields shone a rosy gold in the setting sun. The sky filled with sweeping bands of deep blue and gray – at the horizon a shimmer of pink pulled at her heart. The sad beauty of the day filled her with longing.

Movement from outside the barn caught her attention, and she stepped back. She saw that Otto and the POWs were carrying some tools to the machine shed. From the darkening window she watched them, praying for a glimpse of Friedrich. And then the ache in her heart deepened – there he was – tall, straight, strong – then he went back into the barn. She remembered her hand on his chest, the look in his eyes. He was all seething passion and desire and – she let the curtain fall.

Ursula lay down on her bed, too tired to take off her dress, and pulled the quilts over her. Through the lace curtains she could see the bare tree limbs – she knew they would bloom again in the spring, but now they appeared utterly dead.

He is the enemy, she told herself again. She thought of the day in October when she had first seen him; of sitting so close to him milking the cow, their fingers linked; his hand clasping her arm, her chin; the look in his eyes tonight in the kitchen. "Friedrich," she dared to whisper.

She heard voices and the squeaky opening and slamming of Otto's truck doors, and then heard the gears grinding, and the truck drive off. She wanted to sleep, but her mind was filled with stirring images. His eyes – my God, but they haunt me so. How is it that he leaves the farm – and yet remains here with me?

A heaviness pressed down on her and she thought of her brother Francis, of all her brothers out there in the harsh world. They were not fighters; they were farmers, in love with the land and the rhythms of the seasons. She thought of Joe and his limp, and of the boys at the dance tonight, all in desperate search of love and happiness. She thought of all the sickening horror in the world.

But overshadowing everything was a deep sense of betrayal, and anguish at a problem that had no possible solution. Work, exhaustion, and a constantly stoked attempt at hatred were the only antidotes for the hopeless longing inside her. She felt ill at the churning emotions. No. She couldn't even look at it. It was too awful, too traitorous, too unthinkable.

Sick at heart, she drifted closer to sleep, aware of the growing silence. Peace. Just the small sounds of the end of day: a few cawing birds, the milk cows gently lowing. The entrance to sleep finally welcomed her.

Only minutes earlier, Otto had been checking his watch, concerned about getting the prisoners back on time. Friedrich was nearly finished painting, but it made no sense to stop now – the brushes wouldn't be dry by tomorrow. Better to finish today – another ten or fifteen minutes would do it.

Otto scratched his head and looked around, settling the dilemma by discussing it aloud.

"Can't leave the painting unfinished. Yet I can't leave you all here." He would bend the rules, just a bit. "Friedrich – you finish up. Gustav, Karl, you come with me to pick up the others from the other two farms." He looked around and nodded in approval to himself. "We have to come back this way anyway. Nobody's home. Can't see as it'll do any harm."

In rudimentary German, and with a lot of tapping at an imaginary watch, he explained his plan to Friedrich, miming washing brushes at the pump and bringing them into the house.

Friedrich nodded, barely looking up from his painting, his mind full of Ursula.

Otto and the others hopped into the cab of the truck, and headed off.

Friedrich finished the painting, and washed out the brushes at the pump. Then he took a moment to look out over the fields, and raised his head to the fading sky, grateful for the chance to be alone.

He should have felt free, but something stronger than chains bound his heart. He looked over at the house, dark now, except for the light coming from the kitchen window. Out of habit, he looked up at the window with the lace curtains. He had often seen her standing there, and once or twice had caught her looking at him. But she always quickly moved away. If only once she had stayed there, if only once she had –

He stopped his thoughts, as he had learned to do, and picked up the brushes and paint can. Then he carried them up to the house, and set them inside the porch. The warmth from the kitchen beckoned him; he would wait there until the truck returned. He looked at the archway between the hallway and kitchen where she had lately stood framed, and tried to conjure up her image again. He imagined her moving about the kitchen, and wondered which seat was hers. He moved from one chair to the next, letting his hand rest on each.

Then he closed his eyes. Just being in the space she had lately stood suffused him with peace. Words from one of his beloved lieder filled his mind, so closely did they express the yearning in his heart. *You are peace, gentle peace. You are the longing, and what stills it.*

He could see into the living room where a lamp had been left on. It cast a soft golden light onto the piano and the photos on top of it. He walked into the living room where he had been only a few times. Though he felt like an intruder, he stood before the piano and lifted the photo of Ursula. He pressed it to his heart, and then raised it to his lips and kissed it. "Ursula," he said softly. He felt as if his heart would break. He set the photo down in front of him, and lightly touched the keys. *Du Bist Die Ruh*, he sang in a whisper.

He felt that his pain would lessen if he could hear the words, feel them through his fingers on the keys. With his right hand he played the simple melody, but it only intensified his pain – and yet he wanted more. He sat down on the piano stool and, with his eyes on the image of Ursula, he indulged the pleasure-pain of his heart. While he played, he allowed the silent words to fuel his dream of her, knowing that it could never be. And yet it brought solace to his yearning, to imagine what could have been, in another world, in another time. *Come live with me, and close quietly the gate behind you.* Then, aching from desire and love and longing, he began to sing the words, feeling in some way that he was giving himself to her.

He gave his voice to the melody and filled his heart with the dream of Ursula. Then he stopped. She hated him, or wanted to. There was something between them that should not be, could not be. And she hated him for it. Rightly so. And yet he could not deny what was between them, and he began the song again.

Now, surrendering to the beauty of his dream, he allowed his voice to fill and rise, losing himself, escaping from time and place, from war and pain. *Drive other pain out of this breast . . . . Oh, fill me completely.* Ursula. Ursula.

Upstairs in the fading light, Ursula tossed in a fitful sleep. Weeks of misery and remorse stormed inside her troubled mind.

Then, from some distant place, a simple strain of loveliness washed over her – a melody of such unearthly sweetness that it took away all pain and trouble. A dream melody that answered to her anguish and brought her peace.

She opened her eyes, and realized that it was real music, coming from downstairs. Then a voice joined the strain, a stirring song of words she didn't understand, but knew were words of love. Wrenching words of yearning and tenderness. And she knew it was him; she had stepped into a waking dream.

Then it stopped. She held her breath, willing it to continue, pleading for it to continue. Slowly, it began again, more fully now.

All worry and sadness vanished in the beauty of the song. And she softly smiled at the simple answer, the only answer, to all longing and bitterness and regret. Love. Love that rose above the wounded world and soared high above earth's sorrow.

She sat up, overcome with the beauty of life, of all that is pure and noble and striving. And she understood that the only thing that can heal and connect and lift us is love. The answer to her anguish had been there all along. In that moment, she knew that she would risk all for him. Nothing else mattered. To lessen his pain, to feel his love, was all she wanted. To be in his arms and to feel the sweetness of life.

The house, the evening, the world became imbued with utter loveliness, and she rose, moving in the waking dream. She walked down the hall, willing the music to go on and on; to stay in it, her only desire, to exist in that earthy yet unearthly beauty.

Down the stairs, following the song of love, she approached the room. There he was. There was her love. There, in the golden lamplight, strong, beautiful, his voice filled with longing and love – for her.

The aching words rose, then fell, then rested – and he suddenly became aware of her. He stood so quickly that the piano stool toppled over. Horrified that he had sat at their piano, singing his love to her, her photo there before him.

He remained absolutely still, fearing her words, her anger – until he saw the gentleness in her eyes. He didn't apologize or make excuses or try to flee, but held her gaze, astonished that this time there was no barrier between them.

Ursula walked up to him, and took his hands, and felt all his pent up love and sorrow and passion. Her mouth softened into a sad smile, to see that he trembled before her.

"Ursula," he said, his heart brimming.

The agonizing tension between them finally disappeared, as they embraced and pressed into each other. She raised her face to him, and he brought his lips to hers. The moment hovered in timelessness.

Friedrich gently cupped her face in his hands. "I love you, Ursula. I'm so sorry, but I love you completely."

"And I love you, Friedrich. God help me, but I love you with all my heart." She reached up and held him tightly, stunned by the enormity of her passion for him, wanting to dissolve into him, into all that is tender and beautiful.

A passionate embrace, a kiss made all the sweeter for having been suppressed for so long, was suddenly broken by the cruel rumble of a truck coming up the farmhouse lane; the finely spun dream-world they had so briefly set foot in, now crumbled before them.

His eyes filled with desperate sadness again. "I can't bear to lose you, Ursula."

"You won't. I will wait for you, Friedrich – no matter how long it takes."

In that golden moment, their lives changed forever, knowing that no matter how long the war lasted, no matter what else happened, they belonged to each other, and nothing would come between them.

A flash of headlights as the truck pulled up shone into the kitchen window, and the breaks squealed to a stop. A voice called out to him.

They embraced and kissed one more time, and then Friedrich quickly left as footsteps fell on the porch.

Ursula stood motionless. She heard the kitchen door slam, heard the truck door creak open and shut, heard the truck turn back onto the lane.

She then ran upstairs to her bedroom window and watched the truck drive away from her. She kept her eyes fixed on it as it turned onto the country road and slowly disappeared in the distance.

Radiance filled her face and her heart swelled with wild joy – she had seen happiness in his beautiful eyes, and she knew the strength of his love.

Then her smile slowly faded, and her thoughts became tempered with a more sobering vision – though no less beautiful – for she knew the path she was going to take, and the trouble it would bring.

Chapter 13

In the official bomb shelter for the neighborhood, the basement of the apartment building where Mickey and Billy Kinney lived, Tommy lay wide awake in the darkness – trying not to think of what he had seen that night at the hospital. But the images kept coming back. He had accidentally rushed into the wrong ward. Some kind of ward where things were bad. He didn't know that things could be so bad. Not like that.

He had stood inside the room – frozen. The moans were the first thing that frightened him – they were grown men sounds, new to his ears. Cries, groans, even a scream. His stomach had clenched. But he told himself he could do this. He swallowed and straightened up. He would show them that he would soon be a soldier and would take care of the enemy. He took a step forward.

The smell was the next thing to hit him. He didn't know what it was – medicine, and something else he didn't want to think about. Another step forward.

Then he saw them – broken, wounded, bandaged. Limbs gone, faces partly gone, mouths twisted, eyes full of horror. They were watching him.

He stood immobile – trying to be brave. He felt so bad for them – they were soldiers, but they were all messed up, crooked, broken – it was all wrong, not how war and heroes were supposed to be. He didn't want the world to be like this.

He wanted to be strong and brave – for them – but he wanted to cry. His stomach started to rise. His head felt light, he felt the blood leave his face, and he broke into a sweat, drenched. He backed out of the room, and found the men's room just in time.

The next thing he remembered was the doctor leaning over him. Asking him questions. Giving him water. He was a nice man. Kind, gentle like a mother.

Tommy turned in his sleep, trying to remember the doctor, his kind old face. But those other images, those faces were walking towards him. He was scared to death. Scared they would get him, scared he was one of them . . .

*

Lillian, wrapped in one of Charles's shirts, had barely fallen asleep when the phone rang. She jumped up, glanced at the clock, and rushed into the living room. It was Mickey's mother, Mrs. Kinney, speaking softly into the phone. Lillian's heart began to pound.

"Sorry to call at this hour, but – "

"Mrs. Kinney, what is it? Are the boys all right?"

"They're fine. Gabriel is asleep. But Tommy – "

"What? Is he sick?"

"No, he's fine, but he's more upset than we realized."

"What do you mean? Did something happen?"

"Apparently when they were at the hospital, he got lost after going to the bathroom and went into the wrong ward – with serious injuries. I think he saw some things that really upset him. We didn't know about it until he woke up crying – in a jumble we pieced it together. He said he wants to go home. So Michael will take him. They're just leaving now."

"Thank you. I'll go downstairs and wait for them."

Lillian threw on her robe and slippers, ran downstairs, and opened the vestibule door. She waited at the top of the steps outside, shivering. She soon saw Tommy and Mr. Kinney walking towards the building.

As they climbed the steps, she could see that Tommy was trying to be brave about it and she thought it best not to embrace him right now.

"Thanks, Mr. Kinney," said Tommy. "Sorry."

Mr. Kinney rubbed his shoulder. "No need to apologize, Tommy. I'm just sorry it happened. And you can still come back for breakfast, if you want." Mr. Kinney looked up at Lillian, his eyes full of a father's concern, then back at Tommy. "We're fixing a GI breakfast – spam and eggs, if you want."

"Thanks. I'll think about it."

Mr. Kinney nodded goodnight to Lillian, turned up his coat collar against the cold, and headed back home.

Lillian opened the door for Tommy and followed him up the stairs, noticing that he was still in his pajamas. When they reached their apartment, Tommy took off his coat, went straight to bed, and climbed under the covers.

Lillian sat next to him, stroking his hair back from his forehead. "Do you want to tell me what happened?"

Tommy looked away, trying to figure out if he wanted to describe what he'd seen. He quickly shook his head. "I – I don't want to talk about it, Mom."

"That's okay, sweetheart." She continued watching him, and it seemed to her that he was trying not to see the images in his mind. "Are you sleepy?"

He shook his head.

"Do you feel like some hot milk – with honey and cinnamon?"

He sat up a little and smiled with one side of his mouth. "Yeah. That sounds good."

"I'll be right back."

A little of the worry left Tommy's face as he heard the sounds of his mother moving about the kitchen.

Lillian soon came back with two mugs of hot milk. "Here you go."

Tommy reached for the mug, and then tilted his head, puzzled. "How come you're wearing Dad's shirt?"

Lillian looked down and pulled her robe closer around her. "Oh – I couldn't find my nightgown."

As they sipped on the hot, comforting drink, Lillian described all the things they would do up at Annette's.

"I'll pack a lunch for the train ride, and make sure to include some cookies and fudge. But we'll have to save our appetites, because you know Annette will have a big meal all ready for us."

"I bet she'll make roast chicken with potatoes," said Tommy. "And creamed corn."

"I bet she does. And I'm sure she'll have a pie baked, still warm from the oven. Apple, or pumpkin. Or maybe both."

Tommy's smile grew at the vision. "And this year," he said, "we'll help Uncle Bernie find the tree. We'll chop it down, and carry it back on the sled, and decorate it."

Lillian rocked back and forth, stroking his hair. "And you and Gabriel can go sledding."

"Maybe we'll make snow ice cream."

"Mmm," Lillian nodded, widening her eyes at the good idea. "And we'll make a big fire in the fireplace on Christmas Eve."

"And open our presents," Tommy said with a grin.

"You haven't been peeking, have you?" asked Lillian, in mock worry.

"No," laughed Tommy. He soon finished his hot milk, and snuggled down under his covers.

Lillian set the mugs down on the dresser and kissed his forehead.

"Mom?"

Lillian looked down at him.

"I wish Dad could come with us."

"I know. So do I. Maybe by next year the war will be over and we'll all go up there together."

He nodded, and turned over on his side, facing her.

"Mom?" he asked sleepily.

"Hmm?"

"I don't want you to think I'm a baby – but will you stay with me tonight?"

"Of course, sweetheart. I'll be right here with you – all night."

*

Mrs. Kinney called again in the morning to say that Gabriel was on his way home. Lillian opened the apartment door, and set another plate on the table, across from Tommy. Tommy took a bite of his pancake. "He's just in time."

They soon heard Gabriel running up the stairs, and he burst into the apartment, all smiles. Then his face filled with indignation as he saw the plate of pancakes and the maple syrup and jam on the table.

"Hey! No fair! I just had to eat a GI omelet and soy biscuits – yuck!"

"Don't worry, Gabe," said Tommy. "We just started. There's plenty for you."

Gabriel was soon at the table pouring maple syrup over his pancakes. "We're lucky, aren't we, Mom? That Aunt Annette and Uncle Bernie have an orchard and always send us stuff. Maple syrup and honey and jam."

"Yes, we are, and speaking of the orchard, I have some good news for you."

His eyes grew big and he turned from her to Tommy. "What?"

"Annette called this morning and said that Bernie and Danny are coming to the city the day after tomorrow and will take you and Tommy back with them. And I'll follow on Saturday."

"You mean – we can miss school?"

Lillian smiled and nodded. "I'll work it out with your teachers. A few days won't hurt."

"Oh, man, Tommy. That means more time for sledding and snow forts and . . ."

The rest of the breakfast was spent talking about the big trip, now just a day away. Tommy and Gabriel laughed about things that had happened the last time they were there, and asked questions about Bernie's nephew, Danny, and how old their little cousins were now.

Lillian let the boys play outside with the neighborhood kids, and even gave them money for the ice cream parlor. To have Tommy smiling and happy was all she cared about. She hoped the images would fade from his mind, and that the rest of his Christmas would be a happy one – despite the fact that Charles would not be there.

In the afternoon, her phone rang again. Fearing some new crisis, she jumped up to answer it, and was relieved to hear Izzy.

"I have to stop by work to drop off some paperwork that Rockwell had the nerve to ask me to complete over the weekend. Thought I'd drop by, if you're not busy."

"Of course. I could use your company. I was just going to fix some coffee – I'll wait for you." Lillian was happy for the opportunity to smooth over things with Izzy; she would make sure Izzy knew how happy she was for her and Archie.

Twenty minutes later, Izzy came in carrying a boxed cake. "To go with the coffee. I passed the boys outside and they told me their news about going to your sister's. They seem pretty happy about it." She looked closer at Lillian.

"You look like you didn't get much sleep last night. Everything okay?"

Lillian briefly told her about Tommy, and that she was glad they would be up in the country soon.

"Poor kid. That'll be the best thing for him – for all of you."

Lillian poured their coffee and put a few slices of cake onto a plate. "I'm out of sugar. But I can offer you some honey."

"That'll be swell. Speaking of sugar – here. I brought these for you." She pulled out some rationing coupons for sugar. "You can have mine. I won't be doing any baking any time soon."

"I can't take yours."

"Go ahead. Bake some cookies for the boys. It'll make me happy. Hey, you left pretty early last night. You missed the conga line. I tried to find you. One of the gals at the table said she saw you at the coat check and that you looked pretty upset."

Lillian groaned and put her hands over her face at the memory. "I'm sorry, Izzy. I didn't even say goodnight. I – I had to get away from that man."

"Oh ho! Did Don Juan show his true colors? He's one of the more successful cads, from what I hear."

Lillian blushed at the memory of his words. "I should have slapped his face. I wanted to."

"What happened? Did he make a pass at you?"

"A pass? Izzy, he propositioned me! I can't even tell you what he said."

Lillian's eyes burned with indignation, and then settled into dismay. "I – I just wanted to feel alive again. I was so happy, dancing, talking to everyone. He's a clever one. First he got me to talk about Charles, then he got me talking about myself, my art – and how his sister Sally was an artist. I found out he doesn't even have a sister! The brute. Preying on lonely women in times like these."

"Oh, don't be so hard on him."

Lillian opened her mouth in surprise, and anger, that Izzy didn't see the outrage of it.

Izzy put up her hands in defense. "No, I agree – it was wrong of him, dreadfully wrong. But look at it from his point of view – he's going back to the fighting soon. He's just grabbing at life and love and beauty while he can. Like all the guys. In one way or another."

Lillian thought of young Ernest at the hospital, and Izzy's infatuation with Archie, and all the hasty marriages taking place with the girls in the office – everyone seemed desperate for love. She wondered if it was some sort of counterbalance to the effects of war. She shook her head, unable to make sense of anything.

"You're right, Izzy. I'm just angry that I was so easily duped."

"You're out of practice is all. Now me, on the other hand, I've been around such behavior for years. I just brush it off if it comes my way. Unless, of course, I'm interested."

Lillian took a sip of coffee, momentarily lost in thought. "Do you think such things are different now – because of the war?"

Izzy took a bite of the cake and gave the question some thought. She nodded slowly. "I do. I think the war disorients people. I've seen women – who I know are madly in love with their husbands – have affairs. And I've met plenty of guys who go on and on about their girls, yet end the night with – a proposition, as you say. Crazy."

Lillian shook her head. "My God, I hope it's all over soon. Nothing is clear anymore. Everything is fragmented, broken, confusing."

She lifted the coffee pot, and refilled their cups. "I'm glad to be going to Annette's. The boys need to get away from all this, and run wild, and play with abandon. And I'll be going home. Annette and I can bake cookies, and talk late at night in front of the fire, and watch the kids play in the snow."

"I'm glad to hear it. I've decided to go home for the holidays."

Lillian looked up from her cup. "Is Archie going with you?"

"No. He left for Yonkers this morning. He'll spend Christmas there." She laughed at Lillian's surprise. "It's all over."

"Oh, Izzy! I'm sorry for what I said about Archie. I had no business. If you're in love, and he loves you – "

"No – you were right, Lilly. That's why I got so mad. It wasn't love. I know it. He knows it. I can't take away his chance to find real love." Izzy shook her head. "I kept calling him Red. After all this time, it was still about Red, and longing for the way things used to be."

Lillian saw the pain behind the brave face. "Oh, Izzy."

"I explained it to him." She was near tears but was not going to give in to sadness. "He was so swell about it, I almost changed my mind. I saw him off at the train station." She took a deep breath and sat up straight. "I told him there was some lucky girl out there just waiting to meet him. And he said, then he better go find her. Then he poked his head out the train window and said – 'I'll find her, all right. And when I do, I'll just have to make sure I don't call her Izzy!' And he waved goodbye."

Izzy tried to laugh. "He was such a swell guy. But, no. It wasn't love." She took a sip of coffee, and set her cup down. "I guess I have to count myself lucky to have known love once. We – Red and I – we did love each other. And if it hadn't been for this war – and his being wounded – I know everything would have been wonderful. We were so perfect for each other."

The two friends sat silent for a moment. Then Izzy took out her hankie, blew her nose, and snapped her purse shut. That was that. She shook her head, and took another bite of cake.

Lillian had been observing Izzy, unsure of whether to pursue the topic of Red.

"You know, Red still sends us a Christmas card every year. Just a brief note."

Izzy gave a light shrug. "He does the same for me. Why? I don't know, but the lout still sends me cards on my birthday and Christmas. I don't answer. I figure he's just trying to lessen his guilt."

Lillian hadn't realized that Izzy was still in love with Red. But now she saw it clearly.

"He always asks about you, Izzy. This year it was different, somehow. I felt that he really wanted to know how you were doing. If you were happy. He asked if you had found someone. I didn't know how to answer. I don't know how much you want him to know."

"It doesn't matter, Lilly. Tell him whatever you want. Maybe it'll make him feel better, and allow him to enjoy his married life more. I wish him well. After everything that has happened, I still love the guy. I mean, I still want him to be happy. But I have to keep it at arm's length – or I'll be too miserable. He had – has – some kind of hold on me. Well, I better go."

Izzy stood and let out a dramatic groan. "Oh, *why* doesn't Rockwell go away for the holidays? And leave us in peace."

Lillian laughed at Izzy's ongoing battle with Rockwell – and knew that, for the most part, it was Izzy who had the upper hand.

Chapter 14

Love is resourceful. In spite of the obstacles that kept them apart, Ursula and Friedrich sought, and found, moments to be together. Snatches of conversation, secret looks, small tokens left where they would be found. She had told him that the fir tree below her window, which at seven feet tall was so like a Christmas tree, used to be decorated at Christmas. Before the war. So they had taken to decorating the tree with objects that the other would find – from him, pinecones, branches with red berries or white; from her, dried flowers and small glass ornaments.

On a trip back from town, Kate and Ursula were carrying in the groceries, when Kate suddenly stopped, noticing the decorations.

"Ursula – what's all this?"

Ursula glanced at the tree in a dismissive manner. "Oh, you remember, Mom, how we used to decorate the outside trees at Christmas. I'm just keeping the tradition alive, is all."

Kate smiled at the unpredictability of her daughter. "Well, that's the Christmas spirit, Ursula. And I'm proud of you," she said, walking up to the porch, "that you have overcome your prejudice. I've seen you talking to the Germans with more kindness in your voice. It's the right thing to do. It's what we would want for our boys." She entered the kitchen and placed the groceries on the table.

Shame and guilt filled Ursula. She had always been honest and unafraid – but if anyone found out about her and Friedrich, they would take him away, and perhaps harm him. "Shall I leave the flour out for the baking?" she asked, desperate to change the conversation.

"Yes. Go get Jessica and let's get started on the bread."

They were soon sitting around the kitchen table, Jessica and Kate kneading the dough.

Ursula absented herself, hoping they would assume she had just run upstairs for a moment. Ed had taken Karl with him to town to get a few supplies, and Otto and Gustav were out in the machine shed. Ursula saw the opportunity she had hoped for, and slipped out into the barn where Friedrich was working.

A flash of fear crossed Friedrich's face when she came and reached up to kiss him.

"Ursula," he said, looking around. "We must be careful. We can't risk – "

"Don't worry. They're busy in the kitchen. I had to see you," she said, sinking into an embrace.

They sat down on a bale of hay, where they could see the front porch should Kate or Jessica come out, and where they could keep an eye on the machine shed.

Ursula had a thousand questions. She wanted to know more about his family and his life growing up in Germany. He had told her that he had studied in England and that he wanted to get his degree in engineering; that his father was a music professor and his mother played the piano beautifully. He described his older sister who was married with two children. And one day, he told her about his younger brother, Gerhard. Ursula, in turn, told him about Francis, and then about her other brothers, and her memories of her father. She described life on the farm, and shared her dream of going to college, once the war was over.

They had spoken of what would happen if he were to be transferred. It could be for a few months, or, who knew, it could be for several years. There was no telling what the future would bring. But they could at least communicate through letters. Otto had told Kate that he would stay in touch with them, no matter where they were transferred. Ursula at least had the consolation of knowing that she could write to Friedrich, should he have to leave.

"But you must take care, Ursula. You must not write anything that would – "

She placed her hand on his arm. "I would never be so foolish, Friedrich. I would never do anything to expose you."

"It's you I'm worried about. There are many watchful eyes. I want to know that you are safe, if I am sent away. You would be the object of scorn and hatred if anyone were to find out."

They sat quietly for a few minutes, their hands linked, weighed down by the reality of what they were doing. But Ursula brushed away the heavy thoughts, wanting him to be happy in the few moments they had together. She asked again if there was anything he needed, but as before, he spoke well of the camp.

"We have never eaten so well – not since we left home. Besides, we have ways of getting small things we might want." He smiled at her curiosity. "Some of us buy cigarettes or candy with our script, and then trade with the guards."

"Have you done this? Is it dangerous? What do you need?"

"Just small things that remind me of home," he said, and kissed her cheek.

"Is there anything I can give you? Books or food?"

"We are not allowed anything from the outside. But we are able to purchase what we need from the canteen, and some men receive packages from home. But the truth is we have more here as prisoners than our families have back in Germany. We eat well. We are warm. There is even a library that keeps growing with books and magazines. There is nothing we can complain about. The only thing we truly miss is our freedom. And some have found a way to get a taste of that now and then."

Ursula raised her face, waiting for him to explain.

"A few prisoners have escaped camp at night."

She gasped in surprise and sat up straight. "But we haven't heard of any escapes."

Friedrich smiled. "That's because they return before the next roll call. There's a man in my barrack – he has been out many times, just to walk the woods at night. Just to feel like a free man again."

"But why does he go back?"

Friedrich gave an easy laugh. "There is no place for us to go. We've studied the maps of the United States. There is no way we could make it back to Germany – even if we wanted to."

He waited a few moments before adding, "Except for missing our families, the will to return is not there for many of us. We would just be sent to the Russian front or some other form of madness. Even though it is every prisoner's duty to try to escape – that's as true for your soldiers as for ours – we have little incentive to do so. Especially those of us who do not believe in Hitler. Especially after being here and seeing for ourselves the lies we have been told."

"What lies?"

"So many. We were told that the United States had been bombed flat, that the cities were in rubble, and that collapse was imminent." His face took on an expression of awe. "Then when we traveled through the country, we could not believe what we saw. Such a vast land, good roads, fields bursting with crops, cars on the highways, the people happy and well-fed. We were amazed. There were rumors that all prisoners were being taken through a special route, one that was falsely paved with abundance and wealth, and that the destroyed US was being hidden from us. But we compared notes, all of us, coming from different places, and had to accept the truth: the US was prevailing, and our Germany was slowly crumbling. Many of us understand what is happening – in spite of the SS men and Nazis who continue to perpetrate the lies."

Ursula glanced at the machine shed, at the farmhouse, and knew she didn't have much time.

She decided now was the time to ask him the question that most preyed on her mind, though she feared he wouldn't – or couldn't – answer it.

"Friedrich, are you in any danger in the camp?"

He turned his face away and was silent for a few moments. "Why do you ask?"

"I've heard things. About the Nazis in the camps. And something called the Holy Ghost."

He put his face in his hands, and then leaned his elbows on his knees. "You must never tell anyone – "

"I would never, Friedrich. I've told you that I would never repeat anything you say to me."

He let out a long breath and looked down. "All of us – me, Karl, Gustav – we all said we were farmers, in order to leave the base camp. Only Gustav knows farm work; he told us what to say so that they would believe us. I had to hide the fact that I spoke English; that alone would make me suspect. We are all anti-Nazis. But in many of the large camps, the Nazis are in control – complete with spies and traitors and punishment. We're all afraid for our families back home. So we keep quiet."

A knot of fear formed in Ursula's stomach, for what might happen to him.

"I had to get away from the base camp. I had a friend there," he continued. "A musician from

Munich – a violinist. He was older, and sometimes spoke out against what was happening in Germany. And one night, the Holy Ghost came and – "

Ursula saw him wince at the painful memory.

"They broke his hands. Every finger. He knew he would never play again. His spirit was crushed. He didn't live long after that."

"Oh my God, Friedrich. Please be careful!"

He nodded. "We are safer at the branch camps. Many of us have requested transfers. Some letters have made it out to the International Red Cross about the beatings and – other things. I hope to God that something is done."

Ursula kissed his face. "Be careful. Don't do or say anything that will cause trouble." She clasped his hands and brought them to her lips. "Oh, I hope this awful war is over soon."

"Ursula!" came Kate's voice from the porch. "Ursula! Where are you?"

They both jumped up.

"I must go." Ursula ran out into the farm yard. "I'm here! I was looking for Cotton. Have you seen her?"

"She's in the kitchen, next to the stove. Come inside. We're ready to start fixing dinner."

Chapter 15

When Lillian arrived home from work, she heard Tommy and Gabriel conspiring once again in the bathroom, and her temper flared.

"Tommy! Come out here this instant."

Tommy came out of the bathroom, the bruise on his cheek confirming her suspicions.

"I don't believe it! This has gotten completely out of control! I've told you and told you that I won't have you fighting, and yet you continue to – "

"It's not his fault, Mom," came Gabriel's voice from the bathroom. "He was just breaking up a fight. Honest!"

Lillian looked at Tommy and raised her eyebrows. "Is that true?"

Tommy nodded, but avoided her eyes.

"Well why didn't you say so? Who was fighting?"

"Billy," said Tommy, reluctantly.

"Billy? Good heavens, wait until his mother finds out. And just who was he fighting with?"

Tommy looked down at the carpet.

"Tommy? I asked you a question. You *weren't* fighting with Billy, were you?"

He shook his head.

"Then who was Billy fighting with?"

Gabriel stepped out of the bathroom, holding the ice bag to his eye that was fast becoming purple.

Lillian gasped. "Gabriel!" She stood speechless. Gabriel was always the angel, the little boy who got along with everyone, the son she never had to worry about. She lifted the ice bag and looked at his poor little face.

She led him into the living room, and examined him more closely. Then she sank onto the couch, feeling like the world was moving in directions she couldn't keep up with.

Gabriel and Tommy waited a moment, and then sat on either side of her.

Her first response was to blame Tommy. "You see what kind of an example you've been setting?"

"It's not his fault," said Gabriel. "Sorry, Mom."

Lillian took the ice pack and dabbed at his eye, shaking her head.

"I don't know what to say. Billy's your best friend. What on earth were you fighting about?"

Gabriel looked out and pinched his eyebrows together, then stared up at the ceiling and blinked hard, and then finally turned to her. "I can't remember."

She leaned back and let out a deep sigh. "I wish your father were here."

"So do I, Mom," said Gabriel.

"Me too," added Tommy.

Lillian didn't want to go down that road, and quickly changed the subject. "Your Uncle Bernie will be here tomorrow to take you back with him. What will he think? What will your Aunt Annette think?"

Gabriel shrugged his shoulders high. "I don't know. They might think I fell. Or maybe that someone threw something at me. Or – "

"Gabriel! I didn't mean – oh, hurry up and get ready. I have class tonight and I'm taking you to Mrs. Kuntzman's. I don't dare leave you boys alone." She went to the telephone and rang their babysitter, who was more than happy to have the boys with her for the evening.

Lillian gathered her supplies for class, and dropped off Tommy and Gabriel at the babysitter's.

Mrs. Kuntzman opened the door, wearing a red Christmas apron with a pattern of poinsettias. The smell of butter and cinnamon and cloves greeted them.

"Just in time, boys!" she said. "Youse can help me with my baking. For dinner we have chicken over noodles, then nice dessert."

Tommy and Gabriel smiled at the greeting, kicked off their shoes, and ran into her kitchen.

"Tommy, Gabriel! You know better," said Mrs. Kuntzman, pointing at their shoes. "What I always tell you?"

"A place for everything," said Tommy, walking back and putting his shoes neatly by the door.

"And everything in its place," finished Gabriel, doing the same with his shoes.

Then they ran back to the table where a batch of cookies was cooling. "Bye, Mom!" they shouted from the kitchen.

Mrs. Kuntzman put her hand to her chest, and spoke softly. "What happen to our Gabriel? His eye . . ."

"He got in a fight with Billy – and doesn't even remember what it was about!"

The old woman's face broke into a smile. "Ach," she said, waving away the triviality. "Is that all? Don't you worry. Tonight they'll bake cookies. No fighting."

"Thank you for watching them. Tonight is my last class before Christmas. I might be a little later than usual."

"Take your time. We always have a good time together, me and your boys."

Knowing that Tommy and Gabriel were in good hands, Lillian said goodbye and hurried off to her class.

As she rode the bus to the hospital, she surprised herself by feeling somewhat disappointed that this would be her last class until she returned from upstate. It would be two weeks before her next class; she would miss it.

When she entered the room, she noted the festive atmosphere. Mrs. Coppel had arranged for punch and holiday treats, and cheerful Christmas music played from the radio. The men made a show of being in good spirits, despite the fact that most of them would be there for the holidays.

Lillian taught for half an hour, and then gave in to the party atmosphere and chatted with the men, and answered all their questions. She told them about her and the boys' plans for Christmas, about Charles, about when class would resume in the New Year.

Then she stood and gathered her things to leave. "I hope you all have a good holiday. And remember to practice."

When no one answered her, she looked out at them and sensed that they were hesitant about something – she couldn't quite make it out. "What is it?" she asked, smiling.

Memphis pushed Remling. "Go on. Give it to her."

Lillian turned her head in question.

Remling came up to her. "Well, me and the guys – the other GIs and myself – wanted to give you something for Christmas, you know. And, well, being that we're stuck in this hell hole, well – "

"Cut the bull and just give it to her!" hollered Bushwick.

"Go on. Don't chicken out now," Bull added.

Remling cleared his throat. "Well, Vinnie here does a bit of woodwork, you know, and he made a frame – for this."

He winced as he gave her a package wrapped in paper. "I made it, but it's from all of us. I'm afraid I haven't been entirely honest," he said, sheepishly.

"We made him do it!" shouted one of the men.

Lillian hesitated, wondering at his unease.

"Go head," he said. "Open it."

Lillian took the package but before opening it, she addressed the group. "Thank you. All of you."

She looked down at the package, then up at the men. "I just want to say that I've enjoyed our class, and I want to thank you for giving me the opportunity to teach. I'm so pleased at the progress you've made. Even you – *Rembrandt*," she said, laughing at Remling.

She opened the paper, turned the frame over – and nearly choked in surprise. In the frame was an expertly rendered drawing of her that flatteringly captured her likeness. It was utterly life-like, while also revealing something of the artist's style. The picture could only be the result of years of schooling, years of experience; it was the work of a true artist.

Open-mouthed, she looked up at Remling. "You mean – all this time?"

He gave a side nod and winced again. "Don't be sore."

She stared at the drawing – it was beautiful. She cast her eyes to the group of men. "And you all knew?" By the way most of them avoided looking at her, she knew that they had all been in on it. She had been duped. Utterly, absolutely, duped.

The men shifted around uneasily in their seats.

She looked at the drawing again, then at Remling, and then back at the group – and burst out laughing. And laughed all the harder when she thought of the ridiculous early drawings Remling had made, her patient efforts with him. She laughed until tears began to fall, and she had to wipe them away.

One by one, the men also began to laugh, and finally Remling, relieved to be in the clear, joined in. He pulled out his first drawing of her and waved it around, increasing their laughter all the more.

Lillian dabbed at her eyes, trying to speak. "Wait until I tell Charles about this! Oh, I can't believe – " She placed a hand on her side where a pain shot from laughing so hard – and yet she couldn't stop.

"And you all knew?" She tossed her head back and laughed again.

Vinnie finally came to the front and draped his arm around Remling's shoulder. "Rembrandt here is an illustrator for Uncle Sam – goes on the line to let the world know what it's like out there. He's one of the best, so we thought . . ." He pointed to the framed drawing and shrugged.

Lillian searched for her handkerchief in her purse, and wiped away her tears of laughter.

"Thank you, Sergeant Remling. Thank you all," she said to the group. "I'll hang it in my home and it will always remind me of our time together."

The mood was now veering too close to sentimentality for the group of soldiers, and one of them cried out, "Where's the champagne? That's what's missing in this lousy joint!" and he wheeled his chair to the back of the room where a game of cards was getting started.

One patient rolled up the magazine in his hand and swatted the guy next to him, which was greeted with an insult. Another started crooning along with the song on the radio.

Soon they had all settled back into their comfortable complaining and dark humor. Though as Lillian stood there watching them, individually they tossed her a smile or a wink or a simple nod.

Lillian had never expected to feel so at ease in a group of soldiers. And yet here she was, completely at home with these men. She imagined that this is how it would have been if she had had brothers, and she felt a sort of deep love for them all.

Finally, she said her goodbyes and told them that she would return in the new year. It was with mixed joy and sadness that she left the group, knowing that some of them would be gone when she returned, and that new men would be there to replace them.

She briefly went upstairs to wish the other students a Merry Christmas. Ernest sat in the chair next to his bed, laughing with the young Red Cross volunteer. He was excited to be getting out of the hospital in a few days, and briefly told Lillian his plans for the holidays – though the looks that passed between him and the volunteer suggested that some of his time would be spent with her. Lillian wished him well, and said goodbye to the others she had instructed over the past few weeks.

When Lillian knocked at the babysitter's door, Mrs. Kuntzman greeted her with a tin of freshly baked cookies.

"These are ones we didn't eat," she said, laughing along with Tommy and Gabriel.

When they arrived home, Lillian placed the tin in the basket of goodies she had prepared for the boys' train ride upstate with Bernie and Danny.

Tommy and Gabriel expected her to still be angry at them and were surprised when she clasped her hands in excitement.

"Since this is our last chance to celebrate Christmas here before you leave with your Uncle Bernie tomorrow, how about we use up the last of our firewood and make a fire, and have some hot chocolate?"

"Can we?" asked Gabriel, eyes wide with disbelief.

Tommy smiled up at her.

Lillian nodded and kissed their faces. "And I just happened to pick up a box of marshmallows yesterday at Mancetti's."

Soon, the three of them sat in front of the fire, listening to Christmas music on the radio, and sometimes singing along with the songs. There were her darling boys – Tommy with a bruised cheek, Gabriel with a black eye – singing as sweetly as angels. They both had beautiful voices. Tommy's was deepening and developing a rich tone to it; Gabriel's was still high and clear.

Lillian had noticed a pensive air in Tommy lately, but when she asked him what was on his mind, he just shook his head. Now, as the fire died down, she saw the same look as he gazed into the embers. She knew he was weighing something in his mind.

"Okay, boys, time for bed. Go brush your teeth."

Gabriel jumped up and ran to the bathroom. "Me first."

Lillian took their cups to the sink and saw that Tommy was going through the basket of food and taking some items out.

"Tommy, what are you doing? Those are for the train ride tomorrow."

"I'm just taking a few things out so Gabriel doesn't eat them all before I get there."

She placed a hand on her hip. "What are you talking about?"

"I'm going on Saturday – with you."

Lillian waited for an explanation, but he remained silent. "Tommy, it's all settled. Bernie and Danny will be here tomorrow and are expecting you and Gabriel."

He turned to her with an expression that she had never seen in him before – older, determined.

"I have to go back, Mom. Back to that ward. There's Christmas caroling scheduled there for Saturday. We can catch the train right after it – I already checked the schedule. I have to be there, Mom. I want – I want to sing for them."

Lillian draped her arm around him. "Oh, Tommy. I don't want you going back there. It's too upsetting for you to see."

He raised his face to hers. "There will be some adults with me. I have to do it."

She spoke gently to him. "I don't think it's a good idea."

"I have to, Mom. For me – and for them. I can't explain it, but I have to do it."

Lillian kissed the top of his head. "Well, sleep on it. It's okay if you want to change your mind. But if you decide that you still want to, then I'll go there with you."

Chapter 16

Christmas was just a few days away now, and Ursula was happy about the snow that began to fall. They would have a white Christmas. Ursula believed that the holiday would provide some time for her and Friedrich to be together. Her mother was planning a special Christmas lunch for the prisoners, and Ursula expected to find some time to be alone with Friedrich, to continue their conversations, to be in his arms again.

But now, as she sat at the kitchen table mending clothes, her eyes were fixed on the window, her heart tight with anxiety. It was late morning and Otto still had not arrived with the prisoners. A thousand scenarios ran through her mind, none of them good.

When she finally saw his truck coming up the lane, she tensed even more. It wasn't until she saw

Otto park the truck, and Friedrich and the others get out of the back, that she was able to breathe normally. It had probably been a flat tire or some other simple explanation she hadn't considered.

A few moments later, Otto knocked at the door. Kate answered it and asked him to step inside.

"It's about the POWs," he said.

"Not bad news, I hope?" she asked.

"I'm afraid they're being transferred up north to the canneries, at least until spring. S'far as I can make out, they'll be back to help with the planting. Course, there's no way of knowing for sure." He held his hat in his hand the whole time, running the brim round and around through his fingers.

Kate was silent for several moments, and then nodded in understanding. "I'm sorry to hear it. Do you know when?" She had been mentally prepared for the news and had already planned how to deal with it. She assumed it would be sometime in the new year.

"Well, that's the thing," Otto said, his hands finally coming to a stop. "I'm afraid they leave tomorrow."

Ursula gasped, and they both turned to her at the table.

"I – I pricked my finger," she said, putting it in her mouth.

Ed came up to the porch just then, and Kate opened the door for him.

"You heard?" she asked.

"Yep. Otto told me."

Ed remained on the porch, and Kate and Otto joined him out there. They stood quietly, looking over at the barn, out at the fields, then down at the ground.

The prisoners stood outside the barn, their postures revealing sad resignation.

Ed finally broke the silence. "S'pose it makes the most sense to finish getting the supplies for the barn and sheds. It's ready to be picked up. That way I can finish up on the repairs later. Maybe we can get some of the Cahill boys to help out – they're young, but strong."

Kate nodded and crossed her arms. Though the repairs were on her mind, it was something else that tugged at her heart. The three young men had brought life back to the farm, and she was reluctant to see them go. She had already taken out the lace tablecloth for the Christmas lunch she was planning, and had been going over the menu in her mind, imagining the happiness on their faces. The farm would be so quiet without their presence. She decided then and there to get them back in the spring, no matter how many letters she had to write, no matter how much of a pest she had to make of herself.

"We don't got much time," said Otto, looking up at the sky. "We'll grab lunch in town. Pick up the materials, get the lumber cut, bring it back, and unload it. I gotta get the lads back early today. It'll be a push, but I think we can do it." He and Ed walked over to the barn, and spoke with the prisoners.

Ursula had come out onto the porch. This was not at all what she had envisioned. She thought she would be able to say goodbye to Friedrich, to find out where he was going, and be able to spend a few private moments with him. All that was suddenly ripped from her. She grasped the porch rail, hoping to catch a glimpse of Friedrich, to find some means of exchange.

But Kate wrapped her arm around Ursula's shoulder. "There goes the Christmas lunch we were planning for them. Come on inside. Let's at least bake them some Christmas cookies to take with them."

Ursula looked behind her as Kate opened the kitchen door. A worried glance between her and Friedrich was all they had before the truck pulled out onto the lane.

Shirley had come over in the afternoon and was going to spend the night, and for once, Ursula was glad for the constant chatter and giggling that went on between her and Jessica. It helped to cover her silence and distraction. She tried to think of some way to be alone with Friedrich – but could come up with nothing that wouldn't attract attention. She briefly considered slipping him a note, but decided against the risk.

Ed and the others had barely returned from town and unloaded the materials before Otto was urging them to hurry, as he had to get them back to camp.

Kate saw that all the prisoners were sad to go. They didn't know if they would return, or what awaited them where they were going. She stood on the porch and smiled bravely, and told them that she would do her best to make sure they came back in the spring.

"We baked you some Christmas cookies to take with you, even if you have to eat them on the ride to town." She took one of the bundles tied up in red calico and gave it to Gustav, then waited for Jessica and Ursula to hand out the others.

Ursula had positioned herself close to Friedrich, and when she handed him the small bundle, she linked her fingers with his under the cloth.

Otto then pulled the truck in front of the house and tooted the horn.

A few goodbyes and wishes for a happy Christmas – and they were gone. Suddenly gone.

The snow-covered farmyard filled with silence and cold.

Once the truck was at the end of the lane, the others went back inside. But Ursula stood on the porch, trembling. She watched the truck turn onto the country road, and disappear into the distance.

*

Ursula cried herself asleep that night, miserable at their separation. If only she could have held him one more time, if only he could have assured her once more that he would get word to her, if only . . .

She was awoken by a soft sound at her window. She opened her eyes, and was puzzled by the soft glow outside. It had been dark when she went to bed: the moon was near full, but the sky was cloudy and the night should have been dark.

Curious, she went to her window, parted the curtains – and caught her breath in surprise. The fir tree beneath her window that she and Friedrich had decorated was all aglow! Tiny candles were clipped to its branches, softly illuminating the tree and casting a glittery golden skirt on the snow around it. It was the most magical thing she had ever seen.

She raised the window, and leaned out, searching for Friedrich. He stepped out of the shadows and looked up at her. And in the soft glow of the Christmas tree, for one brief moment, the world was a sweet, enchanted place. He placed his fist on his heart.

She placed her hand over her heart and nodded in agreement. Then she lightly kissed her fingertips and sent her kiss out to him. He did the same, and she held his gaze for what she knew would be the last time for several months, if not longer.

A light from another window caused him to step back into the shadows.

"Ursula! Mom!" cried Jessica from her room. "Come and see what Otto did!"

Soon Ursula heard the commotion of Jessica and Shirley putting on shoes and running down the stairs. Then she heard them all go out onto the front porch. Giggling and comments of surprise and wonder drifted up to Ursula.

"Just look at that!" said Kate, filled with delight. "Otto told me that he had been buying candles, German candles, for them. I guess they put him up to it."

Jessica looked down the lane. "He must have lit them and driven right off."

"Ursula!" cried Kate, pulling her jacket closer around her shoulders. "Come down and see!"

But Ursula had her eyes fixed on her beloved, watching as he crossed the dark fields and headed back to camp.

He turned once when the moonlight broke through the clouds and looked back at her – then he disappeared into the shadows.

When she could no longer see him, she returned her gaze to the softly illuminated tree, taking in the farewell gift of beauty he had risked to bring to her.

Chapter 17

༄

The Christmas hospital show was held in the late afternoon. With trepidation that she was making the wrong decision, Lillian allowed Tommy to participate in the caroling that would be performed in the ward with serious injuries.

It was a small group of older men and women who sang the carols – a few older vets and their wives, and two other women, one of them a nurse. They were familiar with the tragic results of war and had tried to dissuade Tommy from joining them. But he had been adamant and convinced them that he could do it.

Lillian entered the room and stood near the door. She watched as an elderly doctor finished his rounds with the patients. He smiled when he saw Tommy and came and placed his hand on his shoulder and said a few words.

After a round of several carols, the coordinator introduced Tommy to the patients, and announced that he wanted to sing for them.

Tommy moved to the middle of the room, and started to crack his knuckles – but then he became conscious of what he was doing and placed his hands at his sides.

Lillian broke into a sweat on seeing Tommy all alone, trying to start the song. What if he fainted, or got sick, or broke into tears?

But her fears were unfounded.

Tommy stood straight, and in a rich, clear tone, he began to sing "Silent Night." His lone voice filled the room.

Tears shot to Lillian's eyes on seeing him standing there, both strong and vulnerable, brave and humble. She had never heard him sing so beautifully, his voice so pure.

Round yon Virgin Mother and Child, Holy Infant so tender and mild – as if he were delivering a divine message of mother love to all the men who lay wounded and helpless in their beds. She heard the words afresh and was moved by their tender simplicity.

A shiver went through her as Tommy reached and held the high notes with ease. *Sleep in heavenly peace, sleep in heavenly peace.* He seemed to enter some sphere of love and compassion where the human heart is able to reach out and touch the hearts of others.

When he began another verse, Lillian looked around at the patients and was moved by their faces. Some were seemingly stoic, but tears ran down their cheeks. Others gently smiled in appreciation. A few moved their lips to the words. Some listened with closed eyes.

The song ended. Absolute silence followed. Then applause, and a few wiped tears, Tommy's lopsided grin when the doctor came up and shook his hand.

The carolers then sang "Deck the Halls" and finished up with "We Wish You a Merry Christmas," while they passed around Christmas treats. Tommy followed, going from bed to bed, sometimes shaking hands, sometimes shyly speaking with the patients.

After going up and down the aisles of beds, Tommy turned to look at Lillian – and was surprised that she wasn't there.

He said his goodbyes, and then went out into the hall. She was sitting on a bench, holding a handkerchief to her eyes and trying not to cry.

"Jeez, Mom, stop crying." Tommy looked around to see if anyone was watching. "Come on,

Mom. We have to hurry if we want to catch the train."

*

Lillian and Tommy rushed through Grand Central Station, their eyes on the clock as they waited in line to purchase their tickets.

Then they hurried onto the crowded platform and joined the stream of holiday travelers that bumped and jostled their way onto the train.

Lillian and Tommy moved from one crowded car to another, until they finally found two seats together. Tommy slid in by the window, and within a few minutes, the "All aboard!" was sounded, the doors closed, and the train started to chug its way out of the station.

After a half hour or so of settling in – taking his coat off and then putting it back on, munching on one of the snacks, and making a half-hearted attempt to read a comic book – Tommy quieted down and let his gaze settle on the darkening landscape passing by outside.

Lillian worried that he had slipped back into that pensive mood, but whenever she asked him anything or caught his eye, he smiled and seemed to be happy.

She nestled back into her seat. Finally, they were on their way. To her sister's, to a Christmas in the country, away from all the stress and strife – at least for a while. She was glad that a few red bows were pinned between the train's windows, glad that someone had made an attempt to lift the spirits in such dark times.

She looked around at the passengers, and saw signs of the season: a Christmas tree brooch pinned on a lapel, wrapped presents peeking out of a bag, a tin of some freshly baked treat resting on a lap – everyone traveling to be with their loved ones for the holidays.

Here and there, groups of servicemen sat in animated conversation. Others sat individually, looking out the windows, lost in thought. A few slept.

From a group of GIs across the aisle, came laughter and the sounds of playful bantering. Tommy leaned forward and turned his head to listen to them.

"The Navy's got you all beat, hands down," said one.

"You're all wet," said another, waving away the assertion. "The Army's the only place for a real soldier – "

"You're right," interrupted a third. "As long as you're talking about the Army Air Forces," he insisted, setting them off arguing again.

One of them leaned over and pointed at Tommy. "Let's let the kid decide."

The others nodded in agreement. "So kid, when it comes your time to sign up, which branch of the service are you going to choose? Land, sea, or air?"

Lillian pretended to be searching for something in her purse, but was waiting to hear how Tommy would answer. She was sure he would go on about how he wanted be a fighter pilot, making one of the men happy.

She was surprised that Tommy seemed somewhat reluctant to respond.

When the men pushed for an answer, assuring him there would be no hard feelings, Tommy cracked his knuckles and spoke softly.

"Well – I used to think I wanted to be a sailor. Then I thought I'd be a pilot. But lately, I've been thinking, and, well, I've kind of decided that I want to be a doctor – you know, like a field medic or something."

Lillian's heart gave a little clench at his answer and she felt her eyes tear up again. She wanted to hold Tommy tightly and tell him how much she loved him.

The men across the aisle were silent for a moment. Then the one who had first spoken, smiled and nodded. "You're all right, kid."

Tommy's answer seemed to take the wind out of their argument, and the men sat silent for a while. Then one of them leaned over and spoke in low tones to the others: "So, three sailors go into a bar . . ."

Tommy leaned back in his seat and gazed out the window again. Soon a lone harmonica sounded from the back of the car, barely audible over the rhythmic chugging of the train. He leaned his head against the window for a while, and then as weariness overtook him, he gave into it and rested his head on Lillian's shoulder.

At the next stop he sat up, and then stretched out and put his head on her lap, bending his knees to fit on the seat. Lillian covered him with the lap blanket she brought, and soon he was in a deep sleep.

Lillian caressed Tommy's hair and looked out the window at the dark countryside, a few lights showing now and then from a house, a farm. It felt strange not to have Gabriel with them, and Charles, so far away.

She thought of how the whole past year was one of fragmentation, despair, fear, and loneliness. She tried to envision Charles, thousands of miles away, alone in the darkness, and her heart ached for him.

She opened her purse and pulled out the last letter from him. Though she knew the words by heart, she held the letter in her hands to better feel his presence: *The tide is slowly turning and we will win this awful war, though at what cost we don't yet know.* Then she skipped to the words that she needed to read now:

Some nights at sea, under an ink black sky, I begin to despair at the human darkness that envelopes the world. Then I think of you, and seek out a faint star, and I am reminded that there is always hope. Though we can never know what lies ahead, I imagine hope as a tiny flame that we cup protectively in our hands, whose light pushes into the darkness and shows us where to place our feet. Hope is a brave little foray into the future, taken with the belief in goodness and happiness.

Then she read his closing words: *We will be together soon, my love. Holding you tightly, Charles.*

Neither the world at war, nor the cold dark sea, nor months of separation could keep their hearts apart, could dim the bright flame of hope. Lillian settled deeper into her seat, and imagined holding a small candle in her hand, tipping it over to touch the flame in Charles's hand, and then allowing the flame to grow.

And before her lay the vision of her dearest hope: The war was over. Charles was home safe. They were all together again as a family. A fire burned brightly in the fireplace, the mantel was hung with stockings, a Christmas tree sparkled with lights and ornaments. She and Charles sat together, hands linked and eyes filled with love as they watched Tommy and Gabriel sitting next to the tree.

Then, encouraged by Charles's words of hope, she raised the candle a little higher, and peered a bit farther into the future – and had to smile. For there was a darling little girl sitting between Tommy and Gabriel, the three children laughing merrily. It might be impossible, it might be wishful thinking, but that is what she saw as the Christmas night train pushed on into the darkness.

Made in the USA
Middletown, DE
15 January 2020

83241051R00156